Foote Switch

By

Mandel Stoker

This book is based on a true story that took place in Longview & Kilgore, Texas in the Years 1918 and 1919.

Title ID: 4919126
ISBN-13: 978-0692262085

Editors: Linda H. Laminack, Jimmy Isaac, Lula
Johnson, and DJM.
Cover Art: Donald W. Burton

First Printing February 2013
Printed in the United States

Table of Contents

FOOTE SWITCH

AN UNTOLD LOVE STORY

MANDEL STOKER

Acknowledgements

I Would Like To Thank The People Who Encouraged Me While I Was Writing The Story Of "Foote Switch."

Much Appreciation Goes Out To Ms. Linda H. Laminack In Putting This Book Together.

My Parents Vernon and Bettie Stoker Sr...

My Uncle William (Jack) Moss who first inspired me with the stories from the riot of 1919

My Wife Pamela My Sons Shaun Jackson & Son Sheldon Stoker

My Friend and Brother in Christ Terrell Edwards

My Longtime Friend and Confidant Mr. Raymond Hicks

The Special Encouragement I Received From Ms. Lula Johnson

The Support I Received From My Two Sisters Rosie and Becky, Their Children and Grandchildren

The Support My Wife And I Received From Her Mother Mrs. Lottie Batts and Her Sisters Tina, and Phyllis And Their Children.

Introduction

In 1918 just around the end of World War I in late Summer in Chicago, Illinois, a young Negro male by the name of Lemmel Walters is going to leave home for college, and become romantically involved with a southern white woman from Kilgore, Texas, and because of it he would never return home. Meagan Reese, the young white woman he gets involved with, is going to be finishing up her final year of college in Illinois. I will also give my readers a heads up on Meagan's short and empty friendship she would have with another young African American male who was nick-named Jo Jo.

While Meagan was boarding with her room mother, Mrs. Harris. Mrs. Harris would share with Megan a lot of secrets about herself when she grew up as a slave in Savannah Georgia. After Meagan graduated from college, Lemmel Walters would follow her back to East Texas by way of train.

When Lemmel first arrived in Longview, Texas he met a young African American doctor by the name of

Calvin P. Davis and Professor Samuel L. Jones. The doctor and his wife Julia would take Lemmel in to their home to live and they would take care of him as though he was their own flesh and blood. Because of the cruel death of Lemmel by the hands of the white mobs of the county, and the article that was published in the Negro newspaper *(The Chicago Defender)* about his lynching. Samuel Jones and Dr. Davis would take a stand after their lives were being threatened by the same whites who had murdered Lemmel Walters. When I write the word "stand" ... I mean they stood up against the racial violence that was being inflicted on the Negroes in Gregg County. This courageous action would bring about one of the largest and bloodiest clashes between the white men and the Negroes ever recorded in the history of Texas. Dr. Davis and Professor Jones would have to escape the white mob and the local law enforcement by leaving Longview at night after they and several hundred Negro men were forced into a deadly battle over on the property of Professor Jones. On the night and during the early morning hours of the 10th and 11th of July, 1919, the white mob destroyed Dr. Davis' and Professor Jones' home and several other Negro homes and businesses. A few hours later Dr. Davis' father-in-law Marion Bush was murdered by the friends of the local sheriff in the community of Willow Springs or Greggton. There would be hundreds and hundreds of Texas National Guardsmen and Texas Rangers displaced to Longview because of the killings that had taken place there. This act by the officials in Texas would help cause peace and order to be restored in Longview Texas.

CHAPTER

1

Lemmel Is Excited About Leaving Home For College

Lemmel is waking up from a seemingly short nap but in reality he had slept soundly all night. This however would be the last morning he would be able to spend time with his friends he had grown up with in Chicago and his girlfriend Nancy before going off to college the next day, which will be
Sunday afternoon.

This is how the story begins.....

When I got out of bed on this particular Saturday morning I could smell the homemade bread, and the ham cooking that had been brought in from the smokehouse the night before. My mother was cooking breakfast, even though it was still kind of dark outside. All of my brothers and sisters were already up, dressed and ready for breakfast. I didn't like being the one to hold up a meal, so I dressed as quickly as possible and almost ran through my older brother's rooms to get to the breakfast table. Needless to say, they were all sitting there waiting on me when I got to the bottom of the stairs. They were all looking at me, then each other, shaking their heads, mumbling for me to sit down so we could eat. So I scooted into my seat beside my older brother. My dad began blessing the food, and in his blessing, he asked God to protect me from all harm and danger while traveling on the train to college. He prayed that whatever decisions I made at this point in my life that God would be with me. My dad prayed as though he and God had already been discussing my future, which he probably had. I also recognized that that was the love and concern my dad had for me, as I was getting ready to leave home for college and be away from his parents' protection and guidance. When everyone had finished eating, dad and my two brothers went outside to the barn and began hitching up the team of horses to the wagon. Mother went upstairs to get her coat, hat, purse and gloves, leaving me and my younger two sisters to finish cleaning up the kitchen and put the leftover food away. I was trying to finish up my part of the cleaning as quickly as possible so I could catch a ride with my parents. I was going to be dropped off as they passed by my friend Nancy's home on their way to the Post Office in downtown Chicago, which included finishing up the final arrangements with the college I would be attending the upcoming fall and spring semesters of 1919. This would be my last year of college. My brother, Aaron, had to drive the wagon, because my dad's eyesight was failing and not even the most expensive pair of glasses would help. My mother would sit next to him on the passenger side.

Dad rode on a seat in the back of the wagon with me. His diminishing eyesight made it hard for him to drive the team of horses so Aaron was the eyes for my father who was in his mid to late fifties and my mother still in her mid-forties. Dad was a few years older than my mother, but he always seemed to treat her as though they were the same age and he always respected her opinion on everything. Dad loved to tell the story about why he was so many years older than mom. I never let him know that I didn't care about their age difference. All that mattered to me was that we were a loving family, so I sat with him on the back of the wagon listening to his stories about when he was a young man living in the south helping the Texas government start a police force called the Texas Rangers in the area where he lived. He told me that the Texas Rangers wouldn't accept men unless they were white Americans, but he and the captain lived in the same area for years, so the captain made a way for him to work alongside the Texas Rangers as a free-lance bounty hunter. He loved to tell me the stories about how the Texas Rangers would travel all over Texas searching out outlaws and bank robbers and hostile Indians. He told me that every time they were sent out on a mission, the order from the governor of Texas would be to capture the outlaw dead or alive. He told me that the all-day riding on horseback for days in the rain and snow and very little sleep was actually exciting in the beginning, but after 3 years of it, it became very boring, especially sleeping alone. In fact he would say that he resented chasing men all over Texas so they could be hung or risk being shot and killed himself, so at 26 years of age he gave up the Texas Rangers to go home where he met this pretty little 15 year old girl, court her for about a year and marry her. After he had finished telling me this, I then truly understood why there was such a large age gap between him and mom. I couldn't help but feel a little sorry for my father because of the loneliness he had experienced before he met my mother, and the wasted years chasing after outlaws he didn't even know. Because of the stories he told me I knew that my siblings and I had to be the luckiest children on earth to have a father like mine. Listening to dad's story had passed the time & when I looked, I could see that we were almost to the road that led to Nancy's house,

Aaron was starting to slow the wagon down to let me off so I could walk the rest of the way to Nancy's house which was about ½ mile down the dirt road. I impatiently waited until the wagon came to a complete stop and jumped off and said good bye to my family as they were pulling off to head to the Post Office which was about another mile down the road. This would be the last time I could spend any time with Nancy before I left the next day on the train to Chicago and Collins City. The post office would be the first stop my parents would make, and then Aaron would take my dad over to his favorite place which is the sheriff's office. He enjoyed talking with the sheriff about the days they had spent as Rangers, and their experiences. Mom liked to go to her favorite store called the King & Queen Palace. This store was named this because whatever you wanted you could buy or order whether male or female. I knew with all of their town business I would have plenty of time to visit with my girlfriend before they came back from town. As I got near Nancy's, I could see that she was coming to meet me. She must have seen me coming down the road.

Nancy seemed to be just as excited as I was about me leaving for college on Sunday. So when we were finally getting close enough to recognize one another she called out to me, "Hey! College man! It won't be long now, you'll be back teaching the whole county how to read and write." With arms extended, we enjoyed a big hug of congratulatory excitement. At this point there was no need for me to walk the rest of the way to the house because Nancy had met me almost half way from the turn off. So we found a good clean cool spot in the shade and sat down. Not being able to contain myself, I started telling her all about my real plans for the future. First I told her that I was going to finish up with my classes and practice medicine. Then I wanted to focus on some of the things I had seen happening to the Colored people, such as the unfair treatment on the trains with the Colored porters, mainly the fact that the white porters made more money than the colored men even though they both are given the same job duties. As I was talking to Nancy I couldn't help but notice that she hadn't said a word and just didn't seem to be excited about the life I was planning to live so I asked her was something wrong? She just shook her head and gazed down toward the ground. I knew at that point I couldn't continue the conversation with her until she told me what was wrong. I asked, "Nancy what is it, is it something I said?" She finally looked at me, seeming to be hesitant in responding to my question. But finally she responded by asking me the question, "Why do you want to practice medicine and not be a science teacher right where you grew up and lived all of your life?" Now that she had finally come out with it, I now felt a lot better, but I was still hurt and disappointed that the girl I was planning to marry and have a family with didn't feel that it was a good idea for me to be a doctor. I was actually devastated by her response and action she had shown when I revealed my secret plans to her, but I concealed the truth from her about how I really felt about it. I had to try to explain to her all the reasons why I wanted to be a doctor. I told her I had a desire to help people no matter what their status might be in the community because it will come a time when everyone will need a doctor I want to be the one that people can depend on. I told her that the people were too edgy both white people and the Colored people. I told Nancy that the atmosphere in Chicago was too intense and that I felt that at any time in Pine County something very bad was going to happen between us and the white people living here. Nancy never said another word about me going off to college but I knew she was very sad and she seemed to be hurt that I felt the way I did about Pines County. Since she had nothing else to say about what were the biggest plans and the most important decision I had ever made, hurt me even more. I wanted her support if I didn't have anyone else's because I considered her to be my closest friend in the world, but I was learning that even your most closest confidant might not have the same views you may have on life. *At that point, the conversation took a turn in another direction and we began talking about the things we use to do long ago, but my mind was still on the earlier conversation about my new life I was planning in Chicago.*

To make an excuse to leave, I pretended that I heard Aaron and my parents coming back from the post office but I knew it would be another hour before they came back through to pick me up. We jumped to our feet to try and listen to see just how far they were down the road. We embraced one another and Nancy said to me, "I'll see you tomorrow at church." I responded with a shaky grin, saying, "Okay! See you then." As I neared the main road I looked back toward Nancy's house to see if she was still in view. I couldn't see her so I sat down under a huge tree that gave off plenty of shade. I just sat there thinking about her. I was so hurt that my girlfriend was hurt, to learn that I was planning to leave home and become a doctor rather than be a science teacher. It would be over an hour before my parents came back to pick me up, but I stayed right there, sitting under the tree thinking that it might not be such a good idea to become a doctor after all. I was starting to doubt myself even to the point of not even going back to school at all and just marry Nancy and live here for the rest of my life. I had been planning for such a long time to be a doctor. So I stopped doubting myself and stood up to see if my parents had made it close enough where I could see them coming down the road. Just as I was getting ready to sit back down, I looked as far as I could and at that point I could barely see the team's heads moving up and down and the wagon they pulled behind it. It was now about 11 o'clock, and it seemed to take forever for them to get to where I was to pick me up. I wanted to go back home, and just be with my family so I could finish packing my things for my trip to college, but it wouldn't be as simple as that.

Aaron stopped the wagon about 20 feet from where I was standing and everyone began to get out of the wagon. I couldn't help but ask my mom why everyone was getting out? She said that Aaron was going to let the horses rest and cool off for a few minutes before we continued back home. I said okay, but I was so tired of being there, and I wouldn't dare let them know I had been sitting there for over an hour already waiting for them to come pick me up. As the horses stood there resting, Aaron and my father went off in to trees so they could relieve themselves in private. I could see my mother staring at me as she found a place to sit down. She knew that there was something wrong with me because of the way in which I asked her why was everyone getting out of the wagon with a sense of urgency in my voice.

My mother and I just sat there on the ground waiting patiently for Aaron and dad to come back. My mother never asked me or said anything to me while we sat and waited. I knew she would wait for the right time to ask me what was going on with me. I sure was glad when my brother and dad got back to the wagon. Now we could leave this place and go home. My mother told him to help her get on the back of the wagon so that Tex could ride up front with him. Tex was the name my mother always called my father because when they first met he stood about 6 feet 3 wearing his Texas Rangers outfit consisting of a cowboy hat and boots. Once everyone got situated in the wagon, mother turned all of her attention to me and as we were riding back to our place she started asking me questions about what had happened between me and my friend Nancy. I pretended I didn't have a clue about what she was asking me. I turned away from her so I could face the trees, and this way she wouldn't be able to see the expression on my face. She became more and more intense and downright agitated with me and my nonchalant attitude. Mother said, "Lemmel, honey, you know, you're leaving for college tomorrow, so please tell me what is going on with you that I need to know about?" Well I told her I wanted to become a doctor rather than a school teacher.

I figured if I told it to her like that she might not be as against it and so adamant about me becoming a teacher here. I knew my mother wanted me to be happy with whatever decision I would make so she didn't try to make me feel bad. After I had told her my plans, she reached over and held my hand and told me to my surprise, "Lemmel, whatever you decide to do is fine with me, you know that. Just give yourself a chance to finish college, and then you'll be able to make a decision that you can live with." I wanted to reach over and hug my mother but because my dad and brother were riding up front, I knew that it wouldn't be smart to show that kind of emotion and not have a good explanation for it. Now that my mother had expressed to me how she felt about my decision, I was even more excited about getting back to college. I couldn't wait to get home and finish packing the things I would be taking with me back to school for one more year of college. When we finally made it home I went straight into the house and straight to my room and started getting all my clothes together. I had been so occupied with my girlfriend Nancy and my trip back home talking to mother about school and my decision on whether I would be a doctor or not, I hadn't taken time to drink or eat anything since breakfast which was earlier that morning. Since it was after noon, I stopped what I was doing and went into the kitchen to get a glass of water. This would give me a chance to talk to my twin brother Larry, since he was bringing in the material and food my mother had brought back from the store. Larry wasn't a big talker but he would listen to me whenever I had the need to talk to someone, so I told him all about my plans to become a doctor instead of a teacher. I even told him about the plan I had for him to come and live with me in Michigan once I got situated up there I was going to send money for him to ride the train back. Just as Larry was getting ready to respond, my dad and Aaron came into the kitchen to get a drink of water. Larry knew without me even telling him to end the conversation and that we would pick it up later when we could speak freely about the things we felt, concerning a new life in Michigan. I left my two brothers and my dad in the kitchen and went back into my room and continued packing and cleaning my room so my younger sister could move in as soon as I left for school. For some reason on this particular Saturday I had more energy than I had ever had before. I washed all of my clothes that needed washing and found everything I didn't need or no longer wore and put them in a box so my younger brothers Sam and Arnold could go through them and pick out what they wanted. Before I knew it, it was getting close to supper, and I realized I was a little hungry and tired, but still excited about leaving for school the next day. My parents had made arrangements with the college for me to stay with one of the professors at the college. After everyone had finished eating I stayed in the kitchen and helped my mother wash the dishes. She asked me if I was finished packing for college, I said yes with excitement in my voice, but when I looked at her I could tell she didn't feel as excited about me leaving as I did. I refused to doubt myself the way I did earlier that morning after my conversation with my girlfriend Nancy, because I had waited too long to allow negative thoughts to enter in my mind about becoming a doctor rather than a teacher.

CHAPTER

2

Lemmel Conversating
With A Negro Porter

I was the first one out of bed this Sunday morning,
except my mother who was always the first one up in
the morning getting breakfast ready for the rest of the
family. After breakfast we all got dressed for Sunday
school and morning Worship. My dad on Sundays
would always drive the family to church even though
his eye sight was getting worse and worse. My mother
always sat in the cab right beside dad, and Aaron

always sat by the window. The rest of the children would find places on the back of the truck. My twin brother and I always sat up next to the cab of the truck, and my two younger brothers sat on the bed of the pickup. My dad had been a deacon at the church for a long time so we were usually the first family there most of the time. Because my dad was a deacon he would open the church doors and make sure that the church is cleaned and ready for service on Sunday morning. Church didn't start until 9:00 am but we always got there around 8:00am, so while my mom and dad were getting the communion trays ready and preparing for church services, my brothers, youngest sister and I would play church by getting the song books and singing. After a couple of songs Aaron would get up and preach to us for at least 20 minutes.

When Aaron finished his sermon we would pick up the song books and sing until the congregation started coming in. I could see by the clock on the wall that it was 8:50 am, so I went outside to see if I could see Nancy coming, but she never showed up. I couldn't help but worry about her because she always came to church. I began to wonder about what could be the problem. The first thought that entered my mind was that Nancy had taken ill and her parents stayed home to tend to her. All the while the congregation sang and prayed, and even when the preacher got up and preached his sermon, I had nothing on my mind except Nancy. Wondering why she didn't come to church this morning. She was one of the few people in my life who knew about my plans to become a doctor and live in Michigan. The fact that she knew that this would be my last day at home for a long time, made me think even more that it had to be something very serious that kept her out on this morning. This would be the last Sunday morning we would see each other. Church was letting out so I hurried outside to take another look to see if Nancy was out in the parking lot and just didn't want to come inside because she would be too embarrassed to come in so late, but she was nowhere to be seen. I looked back toward the church and I could see that everyone was starting to come outside and go to their same spot and talk to each other for another 30 minutes. I knew it didn't matter how long the Church congregation fellowshipped after service, we, the Walters, were going to be the last one to leave. I understood that my father was the head deacon at the church and some of his job duties were to make sure that the church doors were closed and make sure the preacher was taking care of for the day. On this Sunday I wanted to go home as soon as possible and load up the truck and go straight to the train station located down town.

Finally everyone left so my dad could lock the church doors and we could go home. We all got into the truck exactly the way we had come only this time Aaron was driving instead of my father. They didn't tell me why Aaron was driving but I figured he was driving because he drove a lot faster than dad. It was now about 11:30 am and we were headed home and if Aaron drove like he normally drove we would be back home in about 20 minutes. My parents had planned to leave home after we ate dinner at about 3:00 and head over to the train station. I was already thinking about the Negro porters that worked the night shift and how I enjoyed talking to them and trying to beat them at dominoes and checkers whenever they would break for lunch.

There was a more serious situation happening on the trains that travel from Pines County to the town of Collins involving the unfair pay that the Colored porters were being paid. They would always complain to me about their pay even though they knew that I didn't have any involvement in that particular area, but they knew I was very sympathetic and concerned about the unfair pay they were getting even though I was powerless in making any kind of decision that would change the pay scale. I had to admit to myself that I did like the attention the old men gave me and the respect they showed me. As I began to think about the trip ahead and the experience with the Porters working the trains from Pines County to Collins City, the excitement I felt grew even higher than ever before. This is not the first time I had traveled by train to Collins City but I knew it would be a lot different for me than the last trip I had made. We were almost in the city now, my mother, my dad, and, of course, my brother Aaron, who drove the truck my dad, had recently bought from a company in Swiss County. We were trying to get used to having an automobile to travel in and be able to move from one area of the county in just a short time. The ride on the back of a truck was a treat for me in itself. Aaron always looked out for me even though I didn't confide in him the way I confided in others in my family.

The reason I say that is because he looks out for me and he always tried to get me whatever I needed or whatever I wanted. Before I could beat on the cab to stop the truck, Aaron was already pulling over to the side of the road so I could pick the late August wild grapes that were growing so bountifully in huge clusters on the vines in the trees just before entering the city of Pines. I wanted to pick grapes especially this time because the Negro porters seemed to enjoy eating them. Between my parents and my brother Aaron and me, we could pick two baskets full in only 20 minutes which was the equivalent of 3 gallons. My father told everyone that it was getting close to 4:00 pm, so we got back in the truck and drove on down to the train station located by the warehouses over on

Water Street in Pines. When we got to the train station it seemed as though everyone that worked on the train was waiting just for me, the Negro porters in particular because they were the first to come out to the truck and start taking my luggage off the truck and putting them on the train that was headed to Collin County. According to the clock at the train station the train had another 45 minutes before pulling out. The extra 45 minutes would give me time to talk to the Negro Porters about the unfair treatment and the unfair pay they were receiving from the train company. I didn't want to talk to them in groups because I feared that it would cause too much attention, so I picked out one Negro Porter who had years and years of experience working on trains as a Porter and kind of old and settle in his life as a Porter. When I got him off to himself I asked him his name, he told me his name was Roosevelt Peters but that most people and all his friends call him Roo for short.

Well Roosevelt I said, "Roo is what I'll call you because you can consider me your friend as well." I went on to ask Roo what exactly was going on between the Blacks and whites all over the country, especially since the war seemed to be coming to an end, and a lot of soldiers were returning back to their homes. After I asked Roo about our country, he just stood there staring at me for a few seconds and then he looked all around as though someone was watching and listening to our every word. I wouldn't dare say a word or ask him why he was so hesitant to answer me, because I knew he was just being cautious and careful about what he was about tell me. When he finally started to discuss this with me, I almost chickened out and told him just forget about it because at that very moment I felt like I had been allowed to enter into a secret club or get ready to be given some secret code or something. Not that I was such a strong willed person and sometimes strong headed, I found myself really wanting to hear about life from a well-traveled Negro man's perspective. I will have to say that all the things Roo told me was not necessarily the thoughts of all Negroes that lived in the United States. In fact a lot of the Blacks considered Roo to be an Uncle Tom. Roo said, "I feel like all the Negroes would have been better off if the white man hadn't of never let him go overseas and fight and kill other white men. There's so much unrest and tension between Negroes and whites because the Negro soldier had so much success in defeating the white soldiers overseas by putting their lives on the line and in many cases seeing their Negro friends die on the battle fields for this country." I had to ask him, "Roo do you think the Negro soldiers were wrong for fighting back to protect this country and most of all being given the right to protect himself against other men trying to kill him. He turned around and for the first time with his dark brown eyes looked me straight in the eyes and to my surprise he answered me with a strong almost loud voice, "No!" Right then and there I knew I was out of my league because I didn't understand this Negro man at all. One minute I thought he was condemning the Negro soldier for fighting against white soldiers. Then it seemed like his whole character changed when I asked him did he think the Negro soldiers were wrong in standing up and fighting like all other soldiers from the United States. He just stood there saying nothing just gazing back and forth toward the train station, so I asked him again, "What do you mean Roo? He kind of turned away from me and said that there was humbleness or more of a submissive attitude the Negroes had when they left for the war, but when they came back they, or we as an African American race have become more demanding of our rightful place in the United States. "Lemmel you must understand me when I say that the Negroes would have been better off had they not gone off to war, I don't mean they were wrong in fighting for this great country, or wrong for standing up for themselves against the white people here at this very moment. I heard from the Negro soldiers own mouths that because of the traveling abroad, and the exposure and the treatment they had received from people living in other parts of the world made them feel like they were just as good as any man living on the face of the earth. Just the respect they had received from other countryman has taken a profound effect on the Negro character. I felt when he finished telling me all that, it would be my turn to talk, but I wasn't prepared to respond unless I made up some kind of a lie and told him I understood, but in reality I just couldn't figure why he felt the Negroes would have been better off staying away from the war and never having the opportunity to see other parts of the world and meet other people. Then it dawned on me what was really happening to me, it was my own selfish way of looking at life. I found myself listening to Roosevelt talk and give his perspective on this society and not putting myself in his shoes. Once I did that, I finally understood why he felt the way he did. Mr. Roosevelt Peters was born in the year of 1873 and had the opportunity to see a lot of things between the Negro and the white man over a span of 48 years. Although it wasn't always peaches and cream for the Negro families, he did let me know that he was very proud of the young Negro soldiers who had served in World War I. We had been talking now for about 20 minutes, so we both began to look back at the train station. We could see that people had started to get on the train even though it was still in the heat of the day. My mother was heading my way to come and get me, fearing that her child might get left behind if he didn't hurry up and get on board with everyone else. When she met me part of the way down the train tracks she spoke with a loud voice and with excitement, "Lemmel, come on here! The passengers are loading up on the train!

You don't want to be left behind in Pines County for the rest of your life do you?" Then she started to laugh with the kind of excitement I had had for the whole weekend. My dad and my brother Aaron were standing by the truck that was parked a few yards from the entrance into the train station. My dad saw us coming back and waved us to hurry up, but we still had plenty of time before the train left. My mother and I walked over to where my dad was and mother found herself a good place to sit down while we talked for another 15 minutes. The train was starting up so my mother, without saying a word, came over and gave me a big hug while fighting to hold back tears. Oddly, my dad, who never shows his emotions, grabbed me in a big bear hug & told me to be careful. I got on the train and waved good bye to Aaron and my parents. It was almost 5 by the time I found a seat, and as I watched the flagman outside my window it seemed it would take forever for him to give the signal to the brakeman and conductor to start the train moving. I was about to explode with excitement and the anticipation of traveling on a train to Collins City. This is my second time traveling on the train, but this time I knew it would be a lot different than before because I had a little more insight on how the Negro porters were being treated by the railroad unions, the unfair treatment that is. One of the Negro Porters slipped me a newspaper as soon as I had taken a seat, as though it was a top secret message from the government. I automatically knew that this Negro newspaper was something I had to keep confidential for the safety of the Negro Porters or just the Negroes in general. I wouldn't attempt to read it until the train had traveled some ways out, and I could tell that most of the passengers on the train were starting to lie back and relax.

Some were napping. Trying to be as nonchalant as possible, I took a magazine out of my bag, placed the paper inside and pretended to read the magazine.

There was an article about the railroad unions keeping the Negro train workers from joining the unions. The article explained why it was so important to be a union member, so as I read the article it said that the railroad unions were making a deal with large railroad companies to only promote union members. So in this way the Negro workers who were not being allowed to join the unions would never be able to advance to a higher position and receive equal pay. While I was reading this I became very upset and angry on how the white Unions were treating the Negro workers that were trying to make a living working on the trains, as everyone else was trying to do.

Now that I had read the article, I was ashamed to give the grapes to the Negro Porters as I had planned, because I realized that they didn't need or want my token of friendship. They needed a young educated Colored person that would stand up and speak for them in this mean and harsh environment that the railroad companies had developed for the Negro employees. When the train pulled in to a small town the train stopped so the passengers could get out and stretch and take care of other needs they may have. In the meantime the 5 man train crew would inspect the train to make sure everything was operating properly. This 30 minute stop would give me time to take the grapes to the Porter's break room or to their quarters and leave them there without me having to face them and pretend that everything was okay concerning employment for the Negro employees . After I delivered the grapes I walked back to my seat to make sure all of my things were intact, I stepped off the train to stretch and take care of my other needs. When I was coming back to the train I passed a group of Negro porters congregating and was close enough to hear snippets of their conversation, revealing that they had the intention of walking off the job. Roo wasn't among the group. I saw him toward the middle of the train, putting gear grease on the breaks and pulleys. I approached him and said in a whispering tone, "Roo, what is going on with the Negro Porters and why aren't you back there with them?" He turned to me and took two of the boxes that were close by, and turned them over for us to sit on.

We still had another 20 minutes before the train would leave. Roo didn't seem to be upset at all; he told me how many years he had been employed by the railroad companies and the many things he had experienced during his 26 years of employment with the railroad companies. I was curious to know what exactly he meant when he spoke about the things he had experienced while with the railroad. I said, "Roo; would you like to share with me some of the things you have experienced over the years?" He told me about the times he worked for different train companies and that they all operated the same way when it came down to treating the Negro employees as equals to the other white employees.

The way Roo carried himself, one would have never believed that he once played the role of a train conductor, brakeman, and a flagman. Roo told me that when the white union members went on strike when he was a young man in his twenties, he and some of the other Negroes attempted to start up a union for Negro train employees. The opposition was too strong. So much to the point he witnessed his close friend and Negro co-worker get pulled off a train and beaten to death by a group of white workers who complained that the Negros working as conductors and brakemen were receiving the same pay as the white employees. "Lemmel, after I saw my co-worker taken off the train and murdered, I lost a lot of ambition to be a train conductor or a classified brakeman after that.

These young men don't know what it's like to live through something as bad as that, but yet I keep working here as though it never happened." I listened to Roo with tears in my eyes because he wasn't just telling me a story, he was confiding in me. These were things I felt he hadn't told anyone else before especially those young Negro men he had to work with every day that were constantly putting him down and referring to him as an Uncle Tom because of his humble disposition.

"Lemmel," he said, "I want you to know that I am proud of every one of those young men that are standing up for what they believe in, and some of them just like years before are willing to die for what they feel is right. The reason, and the only reason I am not back there with them is because I am past middle age and I can no longer travel from state to state looking for work on the railroad. Because I know at times walking off a job seems to be the only way out or the only way to try and turn something wrong and make it right." I told Roo that he needed to go talk to the Negros and try to convince them to just hang in there until the government could be made more aware of what is going on the railroads. He told me, "Just 60 years ago the Negroes worked on the trains as slaves with no pay at all but now the Negros are actually paid money to be a train porter, conductor and flagman."

After he made that touching eye opening statement I became more adamant in my quest for him to go and talk to the younger Negroes and just share with them some of the things he had shared with me. Things like being a little more tolerant of racism and learn when to walk, and when to make whatever money you can no matter what the atmosphere may be because the white man can manipulate the environment in a way to make Negroes feel unwanted, breaking their spirits and causing a man to walk off a good job prematurely. I noticed that the passengers had started to get back on the train so I knew we only had a few minutes before the train would leave for Collins City. This meant that there wouldn't be time for Roo to talk to the Negro porters. I knew I had to do something, but what? I didn't know just yet, but I knew it had to be quick. Then it dawned on me rather suddenly that my dad was good friends with the train conductor's parents. I went up to where the conductor was and told him who I was and who my father was but he still didn't really recognize me. However, he did know my parents. This gave me a chance to make up a story about me stopping on the way from home and picking the wild grapes and eating them all the way from the train station. When I told him this he started to laugh almost uncontrollably so I knew my story was going to work. I told him I was going to need a few more minutes. The conductor was laughing and shaking his head. So he told me to take the time I needed. I left quickly as though I was in a tight but in reality I went straight to where Roo was and told him we would be given some extra minutes before pulling out to Collins City.

Without any hesitation, he went to the group of Negro porters and began talking to them about some of the things he had discussed with me. I stayed in the background watching Roo. He seemed to have the commanding attention of all the men who had gathered around him to listen. I could tell Roo was a powerful and commanding man by the way the men were responding to him. I could tell from where I was that Roo was doing all the talking, but I could see two or three men standing off kind of away from everyone else listening, but yet not giving Roo their undivided attention.

Without warning they all started coming back up to the front of the train to let the conductor know that they were still with the train and that they would be working the rest of the night shift. I came part of the way so the conductor could see I was ready to leave and head on to Collins City. Before I could get on the train Roo stopped me and said, "Thanks for encouraging me to speak to my young Negro brothers about their first obligation to man and also their obligation to their families at home." I told Roo to be sure and tell all the porters that I am going to talk to the president of the Railroad Trainman Union as soon as I get settled in at the college. I was starting to feel a little tired and sleepy so as soon as I got back on the train and sat down in my seat, I took my shoes off, laid my head on the back of the seat and dozed off to sleep. It felt like I had been sleeping for only a few minutes when I felt someone shaking my shoulder and whispering my name.

Then I heard someone calling my name again with a low tone of voice but I was in a deep sleep and just wasn't responding to the voice. The shaking intensified even more and the voice got a little louder. "Lemmel wake up the train is in Collins City now!!" When I finally roused enough to open my eyes, I saw Roo standing there smiling, almost laughing at me because of the way I was off into my nap. I sat up and asked Roo, "Where are we?" He laughed and said, "Lemmel, we have made it to the Rock Island Line Railway in Collins City." Roo told me that this was the end of the line for him and that he would be headed back on the next train to Pines County. I told him, "Thanks for informing me about yesterday and especially the wisdom you shared with the young Negro porters on the train." Roo looked at me and said, "Lemmel you are welcome, it was my pleasure and duty to talk to you and to my young brothers.

CHAPTER

3

Lemmel Will Meet Meagan And She Will Tell Him All about Her and Her House Mother

Now it was finally starting to sink in that I was really here in Collins City. As I got everything squared away with my new landlord at the college, I had no idea that there would be a young white girl traveling from Kilgore, Texas named Meagan Reese and that we would meet and my life would never be the same again. Her journey would begin in a small town in Kilgore, Texas, to Longview and from there to Dallas and Ft. Worth, Texas and from there to a small town connected to the city of Chicago, Illinois called Collins City, a large community of Swedish immigrants.

I didn't meet Meagan until the middle of the second semester and it happened only by chance. She and I were the first ones to get to the school library on one of the coldest mornings on record in the Chicago area. I had dumped my book satchel on a table in the quietest area and was going over the list my professors had given the class, when a very pretty white girl of about 22 sat down at my table. I guess she noticed me staring, because she looked back and smiled openly. I had been so busy with my class work I hadn't been able to take the time to make many friends, or talk to many people and I didn't think for a moment it would hurt to talk to this pretty little white girl.

So, just to start a conversation, I introduced myself and made the remark that the semester had to be more exciting for her than the one I was having. She said, "All my semesters have been great, I suppose, because I have such a wonderful relationship with my house mother, Mrs. Harris.

The trip here was uneventful & I arrived here by train to Chicago early Wednesday morning. It was still kind of dark so I had a hard time finding Mrs. Harris, my room mother in the entire crowd, but I finally spotted her because of the large straw hat she was wearing. Mrs. Harris always wore her big hats no matter what the event was. I waited patiently for the train to come to a complete stop so I could get to the window and wave my hands trying desperately to get their attention. Because of the low visibility they never saw me waving, so I just sat and waited for all the passengers to get off the train. I finally got off the train and caught up with Mrs. Harris and the driver. I really had to run, too! When I did catch up to them, I could see the frantic and panicky look she had on her face. Just before I made it up to where she was, she turned around and spotted me coming to meet her. She looked at me as though she had stumbled upon a pot of gold.

"Meagan, come here!! Let me take a good look at you." She stood there turning me back & forth, looking me over from head to toe then she just grabbed me and hugged me. While she was squeezing me she said, "I am so glad you made it back alright! We are going to have such a wonderful time this year!" She began to get me re-acquainted with the Negro man that was with her and helping her with the horse and wagon. I remembered his face but his name just wouldn't come to me. Mrs. Harris and the Negro man just stood there staring at me waiting for me to say his name but I just couldn't recall his name. Mrs. Harris realized that I was at a loss, so she said, "Meagan, you remember Mr.Hollins or Mr. Trent Hollins." Then I said, "Oh yes ... now I remember your name Mr. Hollins, I am so sorry it didn't come to me right off. He smiled and said, "Miss Meagan, you don't have to apologize for not remembering my name. I know that it's been almost 3 months since you have been here, and while you were away in Texas I know that trying to keep up with everybody's names was probably the last thing on your mind."

It was like Mr. Hollins was reading my mind. I had nothing on my mind that summer but coming back and getting my degree and starting my family here in Illinois. The Negro porters were bringing my luggage from the train when Mr. Hollins walked back and met them so he could give them a hand in loading the wagon with my things. I was standing there by the wagon watching Trent and the porters load the wagon, when suddenly Mrs. Harris took a high step and a leaping jump onto the wagon. I stood amazed and in total shock to see a 73 year old woman do what she did. Trent and the porters acted as though nothing had happened, so I didn't say a word and I went ahead and jumped onto the back of the wagon with my luggage.

Trent and Mrs. Harris rode on the front and I would curl up with the blankets covering me up from head to toe trying to keep the early morning breeze from freezing me to death. I could tell I was in Illinois by the cool temperature that I was already experiencing, and this was only August. I must have fallen asleep for close to an hour before Mrs. Harris woke me up as the wagon was pulling up in Mrs. Harris yard. I sat up and looked around the farm as far as I could see, and the apple trees that lined the fences were still there. It seemed as though I just was picking apples off them the other day.

Mr. Hollins pulled the wagon around to the back of the house & stopped the wagon just past the corner of the big back porch. We got the luggage off the back of the wagon and on to the porch and he led the horses and wagon the rest of the way to the big wagon shed and barn so he could unhitch and feed them. When Mr. Hollins stopped, Mrs. Harris just stepped off the wagon as though she was 20 years old and again I was amazed at how spry she was at her age. I just shook my head in disbelief and stepped off the wagon myself. Mrs. Harris told Trent that after he fed and watered the horses to please bring the luggage in so she could show him where to put it. I picked up a small bag and was told that I didn't need to do anything but just take it easy. Mrs. Harris was constantly telling me, "Baby girl, just relax. Trent and I are going to take care of everything." So, being silly, selfish me, I just stood there by the doorway trying to stay out of Trent's way while he carried my luggage upstairs. I sure felt selfish right then because I wanted Trent to hurry up and go so that Mrs. Harris and I could sit down in her living room and catch up on our last spring gossip. I could hardly wait to tell her about my plans to live up here in Collins City after I finished school. I started to unpack some of my things and Mrs. Harris and Trent went outside to settle up on what she was going to pay him. My parents had given me some money to pay for whatever Mrs. Harris needed so I was just waiting for her to come back inside so I could reimburse her money back to her. When Mrs. Harris started coming back up the steps I said to her, "Mrs. Harris, you didn't have to pay Trent your money because my parents have already given me the money to pay for whatever needs I might have."

"Baby girl, I have known the Hollins family for many years. He and his family have worked on this place for over 30 years." So after she told me that I put my money back in my little secret pouch that I carried inside my left shoe. "Surely, you're not going to worry about unpacking right now, are you? You have plenty of time for that. Come sit down with me here in the living room and take off your shoes and relax.

It's only about 7:30 am and as soon as we have a hot cup of coffee and rest a minute, we're going to have a big country breakfast. From Longview to Chicago was a good 2 day trip and I had not eaten much. Mrs. Harris was just like a mother to me because she seemed to just know that I was starving from the long train ride. Mrs. Harris also knew that once I was fed, I'd lay down in that big feather bed and sleep like the dead for several hours. So I just said, "Yes, mother." and went on into the living room and sat down, letting out a sigh loud enough that could be heard from anywhere in the house. Before I realized it, I dozed off to sleep and I didn't wake up until mother woke me up 30 minutes later. She had already laid the covers back on my bed, and had my bath water ready. As soon as I finished eating breakfast I could take a good long hot bath. She managed to do all that while cooking breakfast. I was still amazed at how a woman in her 70s still had the energy and strength of a young woman.

When I had finished eating, I enjoyed a long hot bath. I dressed in the pajamas Mrs. Harris had laid out for me and was quite happy to crawl under those covers for a good sleep. It was about 3:00 in the afternoon by the time I woke up. I rose up from the bed and noticed that no one was in the house except me. Mrs. Harris was out by the barn feeding the two miniature horses she had for several years as pets. I rushed and put my farm clothes on as quickly as possible so I could go out and help Mrs. Harris with the tending of the farm animals.

Mrs. Harris with a bucket of grain stopped me before I could get out to where she was and yelled, "Meagan, don't come out here. You've already taken a bath. I'm almost finished with the feeding, so just go back inside the house and we'll sit down in the living room and have a good long talk and a real relaxing visit." I turned around and went back into the house and sat down to wait for Mrs. Harris to finish up her work. As I was relaxing on the couch waiting for Mrs.

Harris to come back into the house I couldn't help but to wonder about her growing up years and marriage to Mr. Harris and if she ever had any children. Since this was my second time living with Mrs. Harris I was starting to feel a little bit more comfortable about asking her about personal things. Mrs. Harris finally finished feeding of the farm animals and came inside the house. The moment had finally arrived and I would have the opportunity to ask her about her past. She came in through the back door and yelled, "Meagan sweetie I'm going to freshen up and get us something to drink and I will be right there." I replied, "Just take your time."

When she finally came in the living room she had a glass of water for each of us. She sat down in her rocker next to the end of the couch where I was reclining on the couch, and breathed a long sigh. She said, "You know it's only a little after three but it's already been a long day." "Yes, it has been a long day for everyone." I was still trying to get my nerve up so I could ask her about what her life was like back in the state of Georgia and East Texas. She just sat in her rocking chair sipping on her glass of water, looking out the front door. It was an easy silence, so I patiently waited for her to speak. Sipping my water, I finally got up the nerve to ask her, "You know, I can't help but wonder about people, so I wonder, Mother, what your life was like back in the old days, when you were young and growing up."

She looked at me for a long moment and without saying a word she got up from her chair and went back in to the kitchen. I started to get warm and sweaty wondering if I had gone too far by asking her about her past. Mrs. Harris after a few minutes in the kitchen came back and sits down in her chair that was next to me. I wouldn't even look up at her. I could just hear her rocking back and forth in her chair drinking her water, and finally she said, "Meagan baby I don't like to talk about my life back when I lived in Georgia and East Texas because it just wasn't a good period in my life. Then I said, "Mother you don't have to talk about it if you don't want to."

Mrs. Harris would then insist on telling me her whole life history which made me feel very good inside that the fact she would confide in me. She began telling me about her life in Georgia when she was a slave girl living with her mother who was half white and half black. When Mrs. Harris was telling me this I put on the act that this was a normal conversation but in fact I was in total shock because just looking at her physical appearance she could pass for just another white woman, a very beautiful one at that. I did my best to play it cool but I couldn't help but start asking Mrs. Harris questions, and before she could answer one question I was already loaded with another question. They were silly questions when I look back on them, but she may have never revealed certain things to me if I just hadn't come out and ask her about the things I did. When I was asking her those questions she was looking at me just a grinning, almost laughing at some point of my questionings, she said to me, "Meagan, Meagan, baby, just hold up and take it easy I can see your inquisitive mind is running faster than I can keep up with." When she told me that I suddenly realized that I was kind of moving too fast and maybe I should be a little patient and let her tell her story. Now that Mrs. Harris had revealed to me that she was a Negro and grew up as a slave, for some strange reason my mind jumped back to East Texas in Kilgore for a moment thinking about my parents who were white southerners and had no idea that their daughter was living with a Negro lady who was passing as white. At that point I realized that the woman that I was having this conversation with was still Mrs. Harris and my mother away from home no matter whom or what race she was.

I still had to ask Mrs. Harris why did she look so white and not the least bit like a Negro, she told me "Meagan it is a long story why I look the way I do, but I will make it short." She began telling me that her father was a white man who owned her mother and that her mother was his personal wench. His Negro female at night or just any time Mrs. Booth wasn't around. My mother became pregnant with me when she was only 16 years old and Mr. Booth was the father of the baby, I was born around 1845 or 46, and no one back in those days kept good birth records of slave's being born, so sometimes I have to guess at my age." "Meagan baby the main reason I don't like talking about my past life is because of the cruelty I had to suffer from the Negro slaves and sexual abuse I would suffer from the white men who claimed to be my father's friend." Mrs. Harris I ask "why do you say that the men were claiming to be your father's friend?" "Master Booth is what I always called him even though he was my biological father and it wasn't a secret that he and my mother were still lovers." When she was telling me this I was still thinking to myself why she said that the men who sexually abused her were her father's friends. I knew I had to be patient and let her tell her story at her own pace, and that she would eventually reveal to me why those men could be considered a friend to her father.

Master Booth would always loan out his best slaves both male and females to his rich neighboring plantation owners alone the Savannah rivers whenever they were having parties or just any social event they were having. Whenever this would happen, my mother and I would always go because of our fair colored skin and my mother's ability to communicate intellectually with any white person living in the south. She said that was one thing that my father had always taught her, and that was to walk and talk with dignity and pride no matter where you go or what company you were in." Mrs. Harris seemed to be building me up with anticipation on why the plantation owners relied on her father's slaves when it came down to parties and picnic outings. Then she started telling me about the all night parties she and her mother would have to work on the river boats, and sometimes they would be gone for days at a time. She told me that most of the time when they got on the large steam boats that there would be only white male passengers, and they would all be wealthy plantation owners young and old, fathers, sons, nephews, grandsons, during this time in Georgia there were more female Negroes anywhere in the United States.

There would be plenty of us on the steam boats traveling up and down on the savannah rivers. Her father let it be known to all the people living in the Savannah area both slaves and whites that no one was to ever to lay a hand on her mother for any reason. He seemed to really love and care about her mother but for his daughter Nelly love and affection just didn't seem to trickle down to her. I say this because of the sexual abuse she suffered at the hands of his friends whenever he loaned them out to work on the steam boats. Then she said to me while gazing down at the floor, "and another reason I tell you that my father didn't show love for me is because it was a tradition alone the Georgia Savannah plantations that once a year all the male plantation owners would take a three day boat ride on the river and would have the female slaves at their disposure to do whatever they wanted to do with them. He knew what was going to happen to me every time he loaned me out to the steam boat parties. I had so many sexual encounters on the steam boats until I lost count because when I was about 15 years old I became pregnant by one of the plantation owners, again..." baby I had so many men and young boys taking advantage of me I told my mother that I had no idea who the farther was of my baby."

She paused for a moment and then said, "I gave birth to a little boy that looked just like all the other white babies at the time, but because his grandmother and mother were slaves he would be just another slave baby born on Master Booth's plantation. After I gave birth to my baby my mother stood up to my father and told him that I was never to go on another steam boat ride or any of those plantation parties. To my delight and surprise he never traded words with my mother and just agreed with her acting almost apologetic for allowing things to happen to me in the first place.

My father, Master Booth still didn't have a lot to do with me or his grandson for a long time even though he would come in contact with my mother on a daily basis. But, one day when my son was about 3 or 4 years old my father Master Booth had two of his number one male slaves hitch up two wagons and prepare to take a 2 to 3 day trip to a town near the Savannah River. He planned this particular trip just for my mother, me, and my son, and for the first time in my life I was actually happy to be the daughter of a slave owner. It didn't matter that the white people of that time considered my mother to be just another one of Master Booth slave wenches because I knew he cared and loved her, me, and my son very much."

CHAPTER

4

Meagan Tells Lemmel the Story About An African American Male Nicknamed Jo Jo

Mrs. Harris had told me so much about her life while she was growing up in Georgia and living there as a slave. She just didn't know how much I was in shock to hear some of the things that the black females had to encounter and especially her encounters in particular after the revealing story told by Mrs. Harris I felt like a new human being. Deep down in my soul I was wishing I was part African, I guess, because Mrs. Harris had told me that her grandmother was an African and up until her death, she refused to speak a word of English. It was starting to get late in the evening when I heard voices coming up the road to the farm. I got up from where I was sitting and looked out the door to see who it was. I couldn't make out just who it might be but one of the Negro males in the wagon appeared to be Mr. Trent Hollins. The other one I didn't have a clue on who it was. As the wagon got closer Mrs. Harris came back in to the room and walked out the door where I was standing watching as the wagon got closer. She yelled at them, "Hey Trent, I see you brought your helper with you again today. You know it is such a blessing from God that you can bring your helper Jo Jo along with you and work alongside each other while you are still young enough to do so."

Then Mr. Hollins said back to her in a loud voice, "Mrs. Harris I do realize that this is truly a blessing from God especially since he's been away from us for so long fighting in the war overseas." Mrs. Harris was standing at the top of the steps of the porch when she turned back to where I was standing and beckoned for me to come to where she was standing so I could be seen by Jo Jo. They all knew I had never met him, and up to this point I still didn't know his role in the family. She called him up to where we were standing on the porch and introduced him to me she said, "Meagan Reese, this is Trent Hollins III, Trent's youngest son." Then she turned to him and said, "Trent this is Meagan Reese, who will be living with me for the next two school semesters. She is from Kilgore Texas and lived with me last school year while you were away in the war." As I was standing there, wondering to myself what it would be like being overseas and fighting people you've never met or had any involvement with, I found myself staring at Jo Jo because of his small stature in size. I was wondering how he could fight grown men when he looked as though he was only about 15 years old. So to break the silence I asked Jo Jo, "How old are you?"

My words didn't sound right to me but at least I had gotten a conversation started between him and me. He seemed glad to answer my question. He smiled, and said, "I'm 23, but don't let the size fool you, I'm strong as a bull." I couldn't help but kind of giggle and act like a silly little country girl. I wasn't used to Black people talking with the kind of pronunciation and almost perfect diction he was exercising, nor did white southerners speak this way back home where I lived. Mrs. Harris told Mr. Hollins to come on over to the barn and get the horses some feed and let them rest awhile so the children could get acquainted with each other.

"C'mon in the house and have a seat while I get you something cool to drink," and headed for the kitchen to pour up some lemonade Mrs. Harris had prepared earlier. While I was in the kitchen pouring lemonade, Jo Jo came to the door way of the kitchen and asked me, "What's it like to live in Texas?" My back was turned to him so I didn't see him coming in therefore I didn't recognize his voice when he spoke. For some reason I just couldn't get used to this voice coming out of this small Negro boy When I turned and saw who it was that was talking to me I became nervous and intimidated by him even though he was being very nice and respectful to me.

"Texas is a great place to live, especially if you lived in Kilgore, even though in the last year or so a lot of your people have left the East Texas area looking for better jobs or just better living conditions." "What do you mean when you say better living conditions?" I was starting to feel a little uncomfortable because of the directness of the questions he was asking me. Questions I never had to address before. I knew he was hinting at the racial problems that the Negroes were having in the Longview and Kilgore area. I still pretended not to know what he was talking about but I knew exactly what he was alluding to because I, being a young white girl from Kilgore, Texas, had already been exposed to the *Chicago Defender*, a well-known Negro newspaper in the Chicago area. The *Defender* was a very popular and informative paper. I figured he also read the Defender, so I knew he knew all about the racial problems in East Texas. With this in mind, I went ahead and told him that the farm workers, cotton pickers and share croppers were not getting fair pay for their work and also did not receive equal pay for their cotton bales. "In other words, the Negro workers don't have any organizations in that part of the country to act as advocates and speak up for the workers?" Just about that time, I heard Mr. Hollins calling Jo Jo. "Jo Jo," with a baritone based voice, "Come out, son, before it gets too dark to mend this fence behind the barn." I was glad his father called him and yet I found myself enjoying talking with him as well. He walked away to join his father out by the horse shed. I was just thinking to myself, "Ha! That Jo Jo fellow is kind of rude," as I stood there holding two sweating glasses of lemonade, I realized that he had done it on purpose so that I would have to take it to them, thereby giving him another chance to strike up another conversation with me. A conversation I was eager to have. I had had occasion to socialize with several other young men back home, but this fellow seemed to be two or three steps ahead of me all the time. Especially, when he walked over to where the wood pile stood, several feet away from where his father was, giving him a chance to talk to me alone.

This was perfect because I didn't feel too comfortable talking in the presence of two Negroes that I barely knew. When I walked over to where he was he reached out to take the glass from me, and at the same time he was offering me a place to sit down. Jo Jo while taking a seat on the ground himself, he seemed to never take his eyes off of me. After he had finally sat down, he said to me while smiling, "Meagan, I know that you are not used to having casual conversations with young Negro men back home, but don't worry I don't bite, so let's try a different subject." I started laughing trying to pretend that this was normal for young people no matter what color they were. "Meagan will you be taking anything in specific in college or just classes in general in order to become a school teacher?" I was relieved that he was polite and sensitive enough to change the subject. Pretty soon, we were talking about school and subjects and other things that I totally forgot about the unpacking I had to do before I turned in for the night.

It just didn't dawn on me to worry about my clothes. I just wanted to hear him speak or just listen to him talk. His pronunciation of words, his deep voice and the perfect grammar he used were almost too much for me to handle.

"No," I told him "I am not taking anything in specific just all the general subjects in order for me to teach school on all levels." "Have you decided where you're going to teach? Any school in particular?" "Well, Jo Jo, if I go back home and live, I was planning to teach at the Negro school in the county." "What is the name of the school Meagan?" he asked curiously. "The name of the school is Greenville School for colored children and I will be the first white person to teach there." He just shook his head, "Meagan, do you think you are ready to teach in an all Negro school?" he asked doubtfully. "Yes, I think so. I've already talked to Mr. Ned E. Williams, the founder of the school, and he has assured me that there are good people living in the Elderville and Easton area, both White and Negro people. And I've talked to a few of the families, and they seem eager to keep the school operating. With a white teacher, there's a chance that it would mean more money from the state for operating expenses. "

"Now that you know so much about me, what are your plans since you've come home from the war?" He said that he was still going to study medicine and become a full time doctor. Even before he spoke, I was already thinking to myself that this was the smartest young man I have ever been associated with. "Meagan," he said to me, "I must admit to you that I didn't do much fighting when I was overseas. In fact, I didn't do any fighting because most of the fighting would be over by the time the Negro soldiers were ordered out to the battle fields. Our main duty was to help take care of the wounded soldiers and see to it that the fallen soldiers were properly buried.

I then asked him what college he had chosen in order to complete his study in medicine. He told me that he really didn't have a college picked out because the college he had attended before the war didn't have the level 4 classes he needed in order to complete his studies. This is when I told him that he might be able to come and enroll over at the college I would be attending. He then looked at me with a frown on his face and said, "Meagan, you've got to be out of your mind if you think a colored man would be allowed to attend school with the whites, especially in this day and time." "Jo Jo, I understand how you feel but I actually saw a few Negro students last year attending some of the upper level classes, just like the one that you said you were lacking in." After I told him this he was silent for a moment with a thoughtful look on his face, stood up, wiping the grass from his pants, then said, "Meagan, you know something? I believe I'm going to try to enroll at the college you are attending and maybe, just maybe, I won't have any problems with the whites if I just take the three classes I need and keep a very low profile." Just as I had convinced him to attend the college I was attending I heard Mrs. Harris calling me to supper so I asked Jo Jo when would be the next time I would be able to talk to him about school. He replied, "I don't know. It might be Saturday before we come back over here, because it all depends on when Mrs. Harris will need us."

I said, "Just as long as we get to talk before Monday, because that's when registration begins." He said, "Sounds good." He headed over to where his father was working on the fence and I headed back toward the house. As I opened the screen door, Mrs. Harris asked, "Baby girl, do you need me to help you unpack your things?" I was so glad she offered the help I didn't hesitate in responding by saying, "Yes! Would you please help me? I am so tired, even though I had a really good nap. Riding on such a long trip on a train just wore me out?" We finally got everything unpacked and I climbed into my wonderful feather bed, I just drifted right off to sleep. I am sure that Mrs. Harris came in and put more blankets on me at some time that night, because I found myself wrapped up under the covers the following morning. As I was lying in the bed that morning I couldn't help but wonder if Jo Jo was really serious about attending the white college here in the neighborhood or was he just trying to make me feel better about the segregation that goes on in most schools and communities today? Well, I will find out for sure on Monday when registration began. I was still in bed when Mrs. Harris came in to my room and said to me, "Meagan, baby, I got breakfast ready, get up and come on down to the kitchen."

I sat up in the bed wiping my eyes and wondering if I was ever going to get rested from that train ride. I finally found the strength to drag myself to the kitchen where Mrs. Harris was already sitting at the eating table and she had my plate ready as well. As I sat down she asked me if I finally got my nap out last night. I said, "Yes," thinking to myself how tired I still was but I didn't want her to think I was lazy so I pretended to be upbeat and raring to tackle a new day. Mrs. Harris smiled at me and said, "Good" I am glad you are finally rested up from your trip because I am going to take you site seeing down along the beach today."

What a happy surprise! She had planned a day at the beach with me because last year when I stayed with her she never went to the beach and she never allowed me to go. I actually perked up when she told me, so I asked her what time we were going.

She said, "As soon as Mr. Hollins gets here to pick us up, and that should be sometime early this morning." I hurried to finish my breakfast and ran upstairs to get dressed for the trip to the beach, and I carefully dressed in my best Sunday outfit. When I came out to show Mrs. Harris what I was wearing she smiled at me and said, "That is a beautiful dress, baby, but today is only Thursday not Sunday, so if you'd like to go change into something that will be little bit more casual and that way you won't stand out from everyone else." "Oh, I didn't realize." I was a little embarrassed and my feelings were a little hurt but I didn't let on to Mrs. Harris how I felt. So I went back in and changed into my regular school clothes. I was almost changed when I heard voices coming from outside. I looked out the window and saw Mr. Hollins and Jo Jo out by the barn. I hurried downstairs and outside. Mrs. Harris turned and started back toward the house, that same feeling I had yesterday when I was talking to Jo Jo. I was overcome with nervousness and wanting to be on my best behavior.

When she made it back to the house she said to me, "Meagan, that's perfect you look just fine" I said, "Thanks!" I felt so much better after she said that to me but I was still a little hurt from the way she had laughed at me earlier even though I knew she didn't mean anything by it. While Mrs. Harris went back in to her bedroom to get one her hats, I stood by the doorway, and I noticed that Jo Jo and his dad weren't hitching up the horses to the wagon. When Mrs. Harris came back out she told me that we were going to take a ride in Mr. Hollins new car and that we were going to be riding in style today. I asked her did we need to take any food or water. Again she kind of laughed and said, "Baby girl, they will have plenty of food and drinks at the beach and everything will be alright ... just come on, relax and get ready to enjoy yourself." Jo Jo held the back door for me, saying, "Good morning!" I replied, "Hi, Jo Jo, this was a quick Saturday." He kind of laughed and said, "Yes, it did come quickly," referring to the day before when he told me it might be Saturday before he and his dad would have a chance to get back over here. We all got settled in the automobile and I began to have the feeling of going to the county fair for the first time. It was never on my mind that I was taking a ride with all colored people. Mrs. Harris rode in the front seat with Mr. Hollins, and as we were riding along, she would turn to the back where I was and talk to me about all the clothing stores that were at the beach and the different kinds of food they sold there.

Mrs. Harris seemed to be just as excited about going to the beach as I was. When she finally turned around and started to talk to Mr. Hollins, Jo Jo asked me what I liked most about the beach. He seemed really surprised when I told him that this would be my first time ever going to a beach.

Jo Jo leaned up to Mrs. Harris and asked would it be alright if he could show me around at the beach today. She said she thought that was quite alright with her if it's agreeable to Meagan. I said, "Yes, ma'am, it's fine with me."

They didn't know just how glad I was that Jo Jo was going to show me around even though I knew he would probably be the only Negro man on the beach besides Mr. Hollins. After riding for about 3 miles I could finally see the beach and all the people that were there. When we got the car parked I was the first one to get out and it was an over whelming feeling because I had never been around so much water and so many people or men wearing nothing but shorts and t-shirts and women of all ages wearing trousers under their short skirts. To my surprise there were several Negro couples and Negro children running up and down the beach. This made me more at ease, immediately. Jo Jo got out of the car and came around to where I was standing and took me by the hand and said, "Meagan, are you ready for your tour of the beach." I said, "Yes, I am. Which way are we going?" I didn't know if Mrs. Harris knew how nervous and uncomfortable I was when Jo Jo took me by the hand, but I was so happy that he did. The four of us walked down to the booth to pay to get in. Mr. Hollins gave Jo Jo some money and told him jokingly, "Don't spend it all in one place." Jo Jo said, "Dad, there's plenty to do down here besides spend money but thanks anyway." Mrs. Harris told Mr. Hollins to come on with her because she knew of a new store that had plenty of new fashioned hats for sell.

Mrs. Harris turned to me and asked, "Meagan is everything alright?" I said, "Yes everything is just fine" and then she told me that it was 10:00 now and that would give us a couple of hours to wander around. Meet us over by the "Catfish Shack and we'll all go to one of the restaurants and have lunch." We agreed we would, so with Jo Jo and still holding my hand, we walked on down to the board walk. Jo Jo didn't seem to show much intention of giving me a tour of the beach. I watched as he brushed off the bench for us to sit on. I was glad I had brought a small umbrella because it was getting warm and the sun was bright. We sat there for the entire two hours watching the ships roll in and out but most of all we were both watching and hoping we would see an interracial couple pass by.

During the two hours we were on the beach, he gave me a crash course on the political life style in Chicago and it wasn't pretty, but for some reason I enjoyed every bit of it. Even though I hadn't known Jo

Jo but a couple of days, he was really starting to open up to me. He told me about the girl he was going to marry before he joined the armed services that he was madly in love with her when he went off to war and by the time he got back to Chicago she had married another man and had a baby boy. Such a tragic thing for a young heart to endure, I thought. He went on to say, "So, I've been concentrating on my studies ever since. Before I left Chicago the whole city was different. People were friendlier, especially the white people. My dad and I could go anywhere we wanted and we were always made welcome. Now that I've come back from the war, there are more Negroes living here than I ever could imagine and the whites living here are very uptight about this." "Meagan I'll be honest. The reason I stopped here is because the whites at the beach don't want Negroes down in the water like we used to be able to do. We have our own beach for the colored people now." I asked him about the pond on Mrs. Harris place. He told me, "Meagan, I don't think a lot people know it but that pond is my own secret world. Whenever I became upset with my parents or later with my girlfriend I would always find refuge down at the quiet pond. Quietly, Jo Jo said, "Meagan, how do your parents feel about interracial couples?"

"Well, I told him, "You know, Jo Jo, I really don't know because we've never had that conversation," even though deep down, I knew my family would never accept a Negro man in the family, no matter how smart or how educated he was. I noticed the sun was getting high in the sky, so I said to Jo Jo, "It's getting close to noon, I guess we better head on back to the car." He said, "Yes, we better get on back." I thought he would reach for my hand, but since he didn't, I could only assume that he had the feeling I was set in my East Texas ways and I probably needed to be left alone for a while.

CHAPTER 5

"Mrs. Harris" Meagan's House Mother Revealed the Rest of Her Past to Her

I didn't see Jo Jo again until early the next week. On Sunday morning Mrs. Harris knocked on my door to wake me up so we wouldn't be late getting to church. She had breakfast ready for me the way she always did. When I came out to sit and talk to Mrs. Harris before heading off to church she reminded me that tomorrow is registration at the school and that Jo Jo was going to come by and pick me up early Monday morning and take me to the school. I couldn't help but grin inside because this was perfect! Jo Jo could register as well. I asked Mrs. Harris if she thought it was a good idea for Jo Jo to register at the white school and not the Negro school. She said, "Meagan, that decision will be on Jo Jo and his parents. I really don't know if being a Negro at the college would cause problems with the white students" Then I told her, "Jo Jo is supposed to register with me tomorrow." she just stopped eating and said nothing, slowly chewing her food. She looked over at me with a big smile and said, "That will be wonderful if Jo Jo's allowed to attend college there." I said "Mrs. Harris it's getting close to church time so I had better start getting dressed because it's going to take us at least 15 minutes to walk to the church." She said, "Time is really flying so let me get my money for church and my Sunday hat and I will be ready to go."

I dressed in my favorite dress, paying particular attention to make sure my hair was combed just right. Mrs. Harris was already dressed and she was just getting a few things out of her dresser. We walked to church and most of the people there seemed so glad to see me. They were very complimentary, saying how they had missed my singing in the church and what a beautiful voice I had. Mrs. Harris and I made it back home from church about 12:30 pm. I knew Mrs. Harris was happy for me and Jo Jo and I could barely wait to tell her what Jo Jo's plans were concerning his education and his plans on being a full time doctor once he finished his schooling. I would also tell her about my plans to live in Chicago once I finished my course of education for teachers. She said to me, "Meagan, I am so happy for you and Jo Jo on getting your education, but there is a feeling inside of me that is troubling every time I think of you and Jo Jo being together."

I was taken back! This was a little upsetting. To think Mrs. Harris was saying to me because we had never had a conversation about me and Jo Jo being together in fact Jo Jo and I had never talked about us being a couple. I asked Mrs. Harris, "Mother why do you have this bad feeling about Jo Jo and me. This is the first I've mentioned to you how much I like Jo Jo." "I've got eyes in my head!" I see how you two are when you're together! I knew from the first time you two met that he was attracted to you and you were attracted to him. Jo Jo hasn't shown even a spark of interest in any young women since he got out of the army and finding his fiancé married and starting a family with another man. The way he was upbeat and talking to you was a relief for me. I asked her, "Mother what did I do that was different?" She just looked at me kind of laughing and said, "Baby, I used to be a young girl just like you are now, and I would lose myself sometimes when certain men were in my presence, especially those who seemed to be so sure of themselves and talked with a lot of confidence." "But Mother, what exactly did I do that let you know that I was attracted to Jo Jo." "Meagan I knew you were still tired from the train ride from Dallas and Ft. Worth Texas but when Trent and Jo Jo came over you lit up like a Christmas tree. You seem to be laughing and giggling like some little girl at the play grounds."

I hated that I was really that obvious on Wednesday in trying to pretend I was used to talking to young Negro men. Then I wondered what Mr. Hollins and Jo Jo thought about me. I was starting to feel a little bit embarrassed by the way I acted on

Wednesday evening. I couldn't sleep at all Sunday night because I was too excited about registering the next day at school and I was also wondering what it was going to be like keeping company with Jo Jo all day. The next day finally came and I quickly dressed, ate breakfast and went out on the porch to wait on him to pick me up in his dad's car. As I waited on him, I watched as different automobiles passes the house and finally after a while I could see his car coming down the road. I went to the screen door and yelled back in the house where Mrs. Harris was, letting her know he was coming. She came outside and just as he was pulling up she called out, "Good morning, Jo Jo, Meagan told me that you are going to enroll at the school today."

He said, Good morning everyone. Yes, Mrs. Harris, I'm going to enroll today. He escorted me around to the passenger side and opened the door for me. I wasn't used to this kind of treatment back home because I was seen riding on the back of my dad's truck most of the time. As I got into the car he closed the door and walked back up to the porch where Mrs.

Harris was standing. They talked for a couple of minutes before he came back to the car. When he got in, I asked him if he and Mrs. Harris were keeping secrets? I was joking, of course, but his answer was, "Aw, Meagan, it was only small talk, it was nothing really." That certainly piqued my curiosity even more when he said that. So I asked him again, "Jo Jo, will you just tell me what she said." He said, "Alright Meagan I see you don't give up. All she said to me was to take good care of my baby and drive slow and easy in your dad's car. You know, Meagan. I was wondering why Mrs. Harris told my dad to let me drive you to school today.

I was really relieved to hear him say that she said to take care of me. I didn't feel he needed to know what she and I had been discussing on Sunday concerning our mutual attraction. I ignored his comment he made about Mrs. Harris telling his dad to let him drive me to school today. From the conversation she and I had on Sunday I had a good feeling why she had recommended that he drive me to school. Watching the scenery, and letting the wind blow through my hair, I was so excited and happy that he was going to be attending the same college as me. I couldn't help but notice the way he was acting this morning. He was talking and carrying on as though this was a normal drive to the school. I asked him, "Aren't you excited about registering for you classes today."

He said "maybe a little bit, I'm not going to get my hopes up too high until everything is signed, sealed and delivered and I'm sitting in a classroom." "I said, "Jo Jo, you must think positive because I have the feeling that everything is going to be alright." He looked over at me and smiled and said, "I know Meagan, because as long as you're around things can't help but to be alright." "That's a very nice thing for you to say, Jo Jo, thank you." It made me feel really special that his interest was deepening and that he had faith in me. We pulled into the parking lot and I was so excited to see some of my friends that I jumped out and ran over to be surrounded by a giggling mass of young ladies who were all busy talking and hugging one another. We made plans to meet up the next morning on campus to see what classes, if any, we might have together. I looked around for Jo Jo and spotted him leaning up against the car, looking unsure and out of place. I had never seen him looking so unsure of himself before, but after all, this would be something different for him and I had to remind myself it was going to be hard for both of us, this being his first semester at a white college. I was going to have to be the one to sacrifice and limit my personal time with my friends in order to help him with his hurdles, not being sure what they would be. I hurried back to the car and asked, Jo Jo, are you ready." With a cute little crooked grin, he said, "I'm here now, so I have to be."

We got a few side glances and some stares, but we eventually got registered. It took walking the entire campus from one end to the other to get our class info, register and back to the bookstore to pick up our books. Getting back to the car, we were hot and sweaty and I made the suggestion that we take a drive down to the beach and get our feet wet. He looked at me laughing and said, No, Meagan, we've been kind of lucky today, let's not push it." "Push what," I said. "Meagan I have to remind you that there is racial tension in Chicago just like everywhere else and it's not a totally acceptable concept for a white girl to be seen with a Black man." I couldn't hide the disappointment I felt, it was all on my face; he could tell by the expression on my face that I was a little disappointed and I said, "Then why didn't I feel it, if it was so obvious!" He got quiet for a moment and then said, "Does it have to be the beach? I know where we can go and wade or swim and it's a cool place with lots of shade and it doesn't cost anything to get in." "Where?" I said eagerly. "Why, Mrs. Harris' farm, of course!" I said, Jo Jo! That's a perfect idea! You always seem to say the right things or have just a positive outlook on things. Jo Jo smiled all the way back to the farm. I tried to picture the pond, thinking of the things he had told me about the pond on Mrs. Harris place, how it was his own private world when he wanted to be alone and just think. I didn't say anything to him about it. I tried to keep my curiosity to myself.

When we drove up to the house Mrs. Harris came out on the porch and asked us if the registrations went okay and I said, "Just fine, Mother. Neither of us had any problems and Jo Jo got the courses he wanted." She said "Meagan, you and Jo Jo come on inside and have some dinner. I have prepared it just for you two." Mrs. Harris must have known I was starving and so was Jo Jo because we hadn't taken time out to eat, being so busy registering for our classes. After we finished eating,

I thanked Mrs. Harris for taking time to prepare a delicious meal. I helped her clear the dishes away and she said she was going to sit down with a nice cold glass of tea and prop up her feet for a little bit and if she dozed off, that was fine, too.
Jo Jo asked her if it was alright for him to take me to see the pond. I was remembering the way he shared with me a few days before how the pond was his private world whenever he felt he needed to be alone. I was feeling like I was special to Jo Jo. Mrs. Harris said, "Jo Jo, I've never known you to go to the pond this time of day."

He responded, "Meagan wanted to relax and cool her feet off after we had a long day walking all over the campus." I said, "Yes, Mrs. Harris, the only thing I want to do right now is sit down in a nice cool spot and let my feet dangle in a big body of cold water." She said, "Okay kids, but you all be careful because there are still snakes out and about." Jo Jo said, "Okay, Mrs. Harris we'll be careful." The pond, it turned out, was more the size of a small lake. I couldn't possibly throw a rock to the other side.

There were lots of thick undergrowth here and there and a spot that had big trees and a clearing where the sun light barely pierced through the tree tops. It was so quiet down here, and serene, I could certainly understand why someone would call this their private world. I would be most reluctant to share it.

I found a nice place to sit down and he asked me if I liked the spot. I said, "Jo Jo, you couldn't have picked a better spot." He found himself a place to sit down not too far away, and once he sat down, he laid down and crossed his feet with his hands behind his head. Watching him, I could tell he was putting on his best gentleman act for me. I don't know if he knew it or not but I was finding this to be very romantic of him. I asked him did he ever bring other ladies to his pond or his private world, he said, "No, Meagan I never have, you're the first." "Why not?" "Well, this pond doesn't exactly represent the high points or happiest moments in my life. This is where I come when I'm troubled about something and need time to think. I've even spent nights down here with a fishing pole and a fire, just because I needed some time to sort things out." I was curious, so I asked ... "Are you troubled about anything now?"

He looked at me and smiled and said, "Meagan, I have never been happier about the things in my life than I am right now." I sighed. That comment made me feel a lot better. Now it was becoming clearer to me that he really was attracted to me after all. I didn't know whether or not if he knew I was attracted to him because I was doing everything I could to hide from him the way I really felt. I knew that it might be next week or even longer before we'd have a chance to spend time together like this because our class schedules were different, so I asked him, "Jo Jo, what are your plans for this week since you won't be starting your classes until next Monday."

"This is going to be the week I stay home and help my mother around the house, she has got a lot of things for me to do, it seems that a lot of work has piled up since I have been away in the war." I said, "Well, Jo Jo, you know I will be starting my classes tomorrow so I will be in the total swing of things by the time you get started next Monday." I said to myself Meagan, maybe it's for the best that you and Jo Jo to be apart for a while because this way it will give you a chance to start concentrating on your studies and not on a forbidding romance with a colored man that I know would never be accepted back home in Kilgore Texas.

After a bit, Jo Jo got up, brushed off his pants and asked me if I was ready to go. I wanted to say no, but I knew Mrs. Harris would be getting worried if I didn't come back to the house soon, so I reluctantly said yes. He stepped over to where I was and like the gentlemen he was Jo Jo reached down for my hand and helped me to my feet. The more I was trying to convince myself that we were going to be nothing but friends the more attractive he became. As we neared the house, we could see Mrs. Harris outside in the back yard moving around or just policing the area in the back of the house. It didn't take long for her to spot us, we both knew she was watching for us because the way she was just a waving her arms, you'd have thought she hadn't seen either of us in over a year.

Jo Jo went over & kissed Mrs. Harris on the cheek and told her he'd see her in a few days, got in the car, backed out of the driveway and headed down the road. We followed to the front of the house and watched and waved until he was out of sight. I remember asking myself why I couldn't be a colored girl just for a few months. Mrs. Harris turned to me and asked me, "Baby girl, what did you think about the pond?" I said, "You have got the most beautiful pond I have ever seen! " She said, "Thank you, baby girl, you know you're the first girl I have ever seen Jo

Jo take down there, so you must be very special to him." "Mrs. Harris, I know that there's I lot I don't know about men, especially the colored men, but Jo Jo makes me feel like I am someone special." Mrs. Harris told me, "Meagan, it really shouldn't matter what the color of a person's skin is, if she or he is attracted to someone, trust me, color is the last thing on their mind."

I remarked that my family in Texas would probably disown me if they found out I was being romanced by a Black friend. Mrs. Harris said, "Since you're in Chicago and they are a distance away in Texas, my advice to you is to give it some thought. School has barely begun and you don't know what's ahead for you and Jo Jo. You don't have to mention right off whether or not your friend is white or colored. You are a very intelligent girl and I don't think you would do something that you would regret for the rest of your life."

Mrs. Harris still didn't tell me what I wanted to hear but she did seem to understand my situation concerning Jo Jo and me. After I had taken a bath and put my pajamas on getting ready for bed Mrs. Harris called me into the living room and asked me to sit with her for a little while, if I wasn't too tired. I said, "Mother, you know I'll always have enough energy for you."

She went out to the kitchen and brought me a glass of cold lemonade she had made earlier that day. "Thank you, Mother! This is so nice." "You are most welcome, baby girl." Mrs. Harris sat down in her favorite rocking chair right across from where I was sitting on the couch with my feet tucked under me. "I haven't had a chance to finish telling you my story about Savannah and my trek to Texas and on to Chicago. I said "No, you haven't, but Mrs. Harris you don't have to tell me anything that you don't want to discuss." She said, "Baby girl, I feel I need to share this with you because I see so much of me in you, and Jo Jo seems so much like his grand dad.

I got married soon after the Civil War was over to a man named Melvin Harris, a former slave from a neighboring plantation. He wasn't as fair skinned as I was in fact he was a dark skinned man about the size of Jo Jo. We hadn't been married even a year when tragedy struck. It was early one Christmas morning when Melvin and I woke up to the sound of the thunder of horses and men running around our house yelling and screaming like Indians. Melvin didn't own a gun so he jumped out of bed and grab his hatchet off the wall. I was begging and pleading with Melvin to stay in the house and pulling on him, trying to hold him back. Well, a man is a man and he went on outside to confront these men who were terrorizing us.

They all had sacks pulled over their heads so we wouldn't recognize any of them. Before Melvin could react two men jumped him from behind and threw him to the ground putting a rope around his neck. I turned and ran to the back bed room to see if the baby was all right. Travis was eight by this time and he was sleeping through the whole thing. I had my arms around him when they grabbed both of us and dragged us out to the front yard to make us watch them hang my Melvin and after they hung him,' they were planning for me to watch my son die the same way ... I pleaded and pleaded with them to not hurt

Melvin, but to no avail. They hung him right in front of me and my son. I was pleading and crying and hanging on to Travis for dear life, but one of the men took him out of my arms and was putting a rope around his neck when all of a sudden a gunshot rang out from the trees killing the man who was putting the rope around my son's neck.

There were at least five men standing there looking around trying to spot the shooter. I broke loose and grabbed Travis. One of the men ran over to the man that had been shot and was on the ground and pulled the bag from his head. Lord, honey, to my surprise it was a colored man that was killed, and the other men that were there took their bags from their heads and I recognized all these men as former slaves of Master Booth. The leader of the men was holding and rocking the dead man, obviously grief stricken, when Trent Hollins came out from the trees with his gun still cocked and pointing at the them, he stood between the men and Travis and me and told them if any one of you try and lay another hand on these people I'll blow your head off.

Well, they scattered and ran away, all except that one who was grieving so over his boy Justin. I had grown up with Justin. Trent turned and focused all his attention on my son and me asking us were we hurt I told him no, thanks to you. Trent and I cut Melvin down and Trent told me I needed to do my grieving fast because we weren't going to have time to bury him. I asked him who that man was holding Justin over there.

He said that's not a man that's his mother, Frankie. I said, "Yes, she's been planning this for some time now just waiting for Master Booth to go on one of his business trips." Then I said, "Trent, Did you know about what they were planning? I just can't believe you knew about this and didn't let us know!" "Nellie I didn't think it would be this serious. I thought they would just come over here and scare everybody out of their sleep and then go home.

Never did I think Frankie and those men would do something like this." "Well, Trent, I am glad you showed up and stopped them when you did. I will always be grateful to you for saving us." Then he told me to pack everything I needed to travel, because I'll be back over to pick you and Travis up as soon as I can get my wife and our things together for traveling." "Trent, what are you talking about?" He quickly said, "Nellie, I don't have time to explain everything right now, just do it, and I'll explain it later. I said okay and rushed back into the house and started packing essentials for Travis and me. As we were waiting for Trent to come back my mother had heard the commotion coming from my house and come over to see what was going on, she came into the house and saw all the packing that was being done. She could tell I was terrified by the way I was crying and trembling she said to me, "Nellie, baby, what's wrong? Where's Melvin? What's going on" I told her everything that had happened, how Melvin was hung and if Trent hadn't shown up when he did, that they would have murdered me and Travis.

She asked me, "Why are you packing? Where are you going?" I said, "Trent has gone to pack up and get his wife and he's coming back over to pick me and Travis up so we can leave the country." "Leave the country!" she whispered. I said, "Yes, but Mama, I don't know all the details so there's nothing else I can tell you concerning the trip." She reminded me that I was with child, and asked, "Nellie, child, how are you going to survive with no man to take care of you and Travis?" I said "I will make away with the help of the Lord." "Leave Travis with me for a while, at least, until you get settled where you're going. I didn't want to do it but I knew it was for the best. Trent made it back over to the house with his wife packed and ready to travel, he loaded all my things on to the wagon. When he finished loading the wagon he began telling my mother that he had figured out the best place for us to go was to a town in East Texas called Nacogdoches, where there was plenty of work for freed slaves. My mother seemed to be a little relieved after Trent told her that, but I could tell she was still worried about me leaving. So we hugged and kissed one another, my mother and me, and I took my son Travis and hugged and kissed him and told him I loved him and that I was coming back to get him as soon as we made it to East Texas and settled down there. I gave birth to a little boy in July of the year 1871. I had no way of taking care of the baby, so my friends, Trent and his wife Ann adopted the baby, named him Trent and raised him as their son. All three of us knew that it wouldn't be smart for me to have a colored baby because I was a colored woman in a white woman's body. The Hollins' couldn't have children of their own so they gladly took Trent in as their own. Oh my, I said, totally astonished, "You mean to tell me that Trent Hollins is your son?" She said, "Yes, baby, he is." "Then that means that Jo Jo is your grandson!" Nodding her head and saying, "Yes, he is." Then she went on to tell me that old man Hollins was killed involving a tree accident while he and Trent were out cutting cross ties for the railroad. This was devastating to Trent so he came home one day after work and told his wife Rita that all of us were going to move to Chicago and that he had had enough of working long hours and in unsafe conditions, that was in 1889 and I have been here ever since.

CHAPTER

6

Excitement Turn Tragic At Mrs. Harris' Pond

Monday morning came bright and early, the first day that Jo Jo would be attending college at the white school. I was so tense, hoping that everything would go smoothly for him. When he came to pick me up, after listening to Mrs. Harris stories, I looked at him and knew that this was a special person that had come into my life. As we were riding to school in his dad's car I noticed that he wasn't very talkative at all, in fact we would go through moments of complete silence. I asked him if there was anything wrong, and he said nothing. Unconvinced, I said, "Jo Jo something has got to be wrong because you haven't said a word to me since we left the house." He glanced over at me and said, "It's my mother. She's been in bed with a high fever for the last five days and the doctors don't know what to do in order to get the fever down, so that's probably why I seem so preoccupied I am sorry if I made you feel I was ignoring you." "Oh dear, you don't have to apologize to me because I understand." He said he knew I did. " Now I was even more concerned about his first day at the college, because I knew he wasn't himself or at his best. So I told him no matter how his day went, I'll be there for you at the end of the day. We'd made it to the school by that time and as he pulled the car up to park and turn off the key, he turned to me and said, "Meagan, you don't know how much that means to me and that is something I will hold on to for the rest of the day." I noticed several students watching us, so Jo Jo didn't come over to my side and let me out and I was glad he didn't because I didn't want the people at the school to get the wrong idea, even though we were getting close to each other.

Finally at the end of his first day at the college, Jo Jo came out to the car where I was waiting for him and I was anticipating the news on how his day went, I could hardly wait to ask him how everything went, but I refused to ask him anything about the school once he had made it to the car, I just said hi and he smiled. I could tell everything went well for him because of the bounce he had in his step and the way he said hi to me with that upbeat tone of voice of his. When we got in the car I asked him did he think about his mother a lot today. He said yes, as a matter of fact I was thinking about her all day. I told him, "If you want to go straight home I can walk home today and you can go home and see about your mother." He said, "No, Meagan I don't mind because it's an honor for me to take you home in fact that's one of the things I have been looking forward to doing all day." I then said "okay Jo Jo "So he backed out and headed down the road where I lived.

When we pulled up to the house Mrs. Harris was waiting there on the porch and before he could stop the car she was yelling for Jo Jo to hurry on up and get home because his dad had been over today and told her his mother was very ill. I had just barely gotten my feet on the ground and Jo Jo sped off in the direction of his house without even saying goodbye. I remarked, "Something terrible must have happened and I would greatly appreciate being told what was going on that Jo Jo had to leave so quickly." She said, "Come on in the house and put your things on the front table and have a seat. I started to brace myself for some bad news. I said, "What is it, mother?" She said, "Rita, Jo Jo's mother died this morning right after Jo Jo came by and picked you up for school." From the look on Mrs. Harris face I could see where she had been crying all day because her eyes were puffy and her nose was red like she had a bad cold. I asked Mrs. Harris when the funeral was going to be she said that Trent didn't tell her because it was too early. She said more than likely, it will probably be Wednesday. I said, "Mother, I really want to go to the funeral and be there for Jo

Jo." Don't worry, baby girl, we will be there if it be the Lords will."

It turned out that the funeral was on Wednesday at 11:00 that morning. While I was at school on Tuesday, Trent and Jo Jo came over to the house to visit mother and do a little work for her around the yard. She told me that Jo Jo had asked her if I was coming to the funeral, she said she told him, of course she is coming. "How were we going to get to the funeral tomorrow?" She said that Jo Jo was going to drive his dad's car over early that morning around 8:00 and pick us up. I didn't wait for the next morning to get ready for the funeral. I went and started going through my best Sunday dresses until I found one that might be appropriate. It was around 8:30 and I told Mrs. Harris that I was going to go to bed because I felt that it was going to be a long day tomorrow.

When I woke up the next morning Mrs. Harris was already up and dressed and had my breakfast on the table. It was almost 7:00 so I quickly ate so I could take my time getting dressed for the funeral but even at a time like this I was still getting dressed for Jo Jo.

By the time I had finished dressing and making sure I looked perfect, Jo Jo was driving up to the house, I looked at the clock on the wall and it was showing 7:45. Mrs. Harris was calling me downstairs, that Jo Jo was here to pick us up.

"He's a little early, but that's better than being late. Mrs. Harris had mentioned wanting to spend time with her son Trent and his departed wife, Rita before all the other folks began arriving at the church. When Jo Jo got out of the car and started toward the house, Mrs. Harris went out and met him hugging him and consoling him. I stayed on the porch watching them kind of in a trance. Jo Jo looked like he had just lost his best friend. He made his way up the steps to where I was and I reached out and gave him a big hug. I knew I couldn't bring his mother back or ever take her place but I was going to be there for him when he needed me and let him know I cared. After the funeral Jo Jo and I didn't see each other a whole lot other than times I would see him in school, I knew he still cared for me but we just didn't find the time to spend together once we started our classes for school. The whole fall semester went by and I longed for him to come take me to the pond, but he didn't come. Mrs. Harris and I saw him going down there a number of times all alone, but he didn't venture close to the house.

He finally came by the house with his dad during the Christmas holidays, I was glad to see him and I knew Mrs. Harris was delighted to see her favorite grandson. I said, "Jo Jo, where have you been we were beginning to think you didn't care for us anymore." He laughed and came in out of the weather and I took his coat and hung it up for him. I said, "Now that the semester is over, how did everything go for you? I know you made good grades!" Jo Jo's face lit up and he said, "Great! I made all excellent marks and my professor told me if I have another semester like this one he was going to recommend me to the University of Illinois Medical Program!." "And that's just what happened! So, Lemmel, that's how my fall semester went." I just looked at her and said, "Well ... that's one of the most beautiful and interesting stories I have ever heard." And then I said something that seemed strange even for me to say, but it seemed appropriate at the time ... "The Bible is so true because life is but a vapor... it appears for a little while and soon vanishes away."

She then said, "Lemmel, you're right because everything happened so fast and then here I am in the middle of this semester and already close to spring break. It seems as though those conversations with Mrs. Harris and Jo Jo took place years ago." It ran through my mind that I'd better get busy if I was going to get some of the biology books before they were all checked out, but I was curious to know why Meagan was at the library so early in the morning, so I asked her, "Meagan, why are you here so early?" She told me that this was part of her work study or her campus job duties for this semester. I told her I had to go and hoped to see her on campus, and she smiled back, "It's not that big a campus now is it?"

I found the books I wanted after checking in the previous books and got them checked out and for the next few days, concentrated on memorizing anatomy. Thoughts of her broke through my mind, the way the conversation we had was easy, and how the words we spoke flowed so naturally. I couldn't wait until I had another chance to see her again. I was hoping that I would see her at the library, but as luck would have it, that chance didn't arrive until early Friday morning.

When I got to school on Friday morning the campus library was the first place I needed to go to check in the books I didn't need any more. I thought that if I went to the library early that there might be a chance to catch her there. Maybe there wouldn't be a lot of students around and Meagan and I would be a little bit more comfortable talking to each other.

I finally got to the library and was delighted to see only a few students at the study tables. I found a good table and offered to give her a hand with the wood she was gathering to put in the wood burning stove so that the library could be warm for the other students. She said, "Hi Lemmel, thanks for the offer, it won't be too long before the other students come in." Once we got all the heaters going, it began to warm up nicely, especially after we had nearly exhausted ourselves blowing on the wood to get it burning. She asked me what was I going to be doing tomorrow or Saturday. I said, "Nothing other than my school work." "Well, if it doesn't interfere with your studies, I would like to invite you to lunch tomorrow so you can meet my room mother, Mrs. Harris."

It all seemed like a dream; I couldn't believe a young white woman was inviting me, a young Negro man to lunch. I was so excited as soon as she told me how to get to her house and the time of lunch, I quickly left before she could change her mind. Meagan had already told me the story about Mrs. Harris so I was already aware of the fact that I would be meeting a Negro woman who looked like a white woman. I would take time off from my studies this particular weekend and think of nothing but Meagan and try to figure out why she invited me to lunch. I had to be careful because of the mean way some of the white citizens treated Negroes. I would pretend to be just another Negro boy going down to Mrs. Harris house to do chores for her. When I finally made it up to Mrs. Harris house Meagan was outside even though it was very cold, she beckons me on, reassuring me that I was at the right house and that everything was going to be okay.

When we walked into the house I saw an older white woman coming out of the kitchen wearing an apron and carrying a cup of tea. I was standing there waiting for Mrs. Harris to come out so I could finally meet her and judge for myself whether or not she could pass for a white woman. The white lady came to me smiling and said, "You must be Lemmel Walters." I said, "Yes." Then she said, "I'm Nellie Harris, Meagan's room mother. Won't you have a seat? Lunch will be ready in a few minutes."
Meagan took my coat to hang up in the closet. I couldn't help but think to myself that if Meagan hadn't told me the story about Mrs. Harris I never would have guessed that she was a former Negro slave. As I relaxed on the couch, waiting, Meagan came back in the room, and so did Mrs. Harris. I was looking at them both but, I couldn't think of anything to say, so Meagan broke the ice and started telling Mrs. Harris that I was the Negro doctor she had told her about. I quickly interrupted her and said I am not a doctor yet

and that I have got a long ways to go, Meagan said, "Lemmel, you have got to have more faith and confidence in yourself. I noticed the way you came to the library early in the mornings determined to be the first one to check out all those biology books."

Mrs. Harris made me feel even more confident when she told me that I had the looks of a doctor and just keep your faith in God and that I was going to be just fine. Mrs. Harris went back into the kitchen to check on the food, and after being in there for a few minutes she called for Meagan. After sitting there for a few minutes they started bringing food out to the dining table and we all sat down and ate a lunch prepared for a king. It tasted like a feast to me, after all the months of eating my own afternoon; Meagan suggested that we go for a walk down by the pond. It was all iced up and just so picturesque, she wanted me to see her winter wonderland.

I was delighted, even though it was still blistering cold outside, it didn't matter to me. All I wanted to do was to spend some time getting to know Meagan a little better. As we were walking down by the pond Meagan told me how her friend, JoJo used the pond to isolate himself, come down here to spend time alone and just think, but he was drowning in his sorrows.

I stopped her and told her that I hoped that the pond was going to be a happy time for us. Then she just stared at me for a moment and said, "Lemmel, I hope you are right." I didn't dare comment on what she said, but I knew at that moment that she had been hurt by Jo Jo. I could tell by the way she talked and carried herself that she wasn't afraid to open up and talk to people. This made it easier on me because I wasn't used to talking to white woman in this kind of way either. We stayed at the pond for a long time, talking about the life styles in Kilgore and about her siblings and friends back home. At 4:30 we decided to head on back to the house. We decided that the pond would become our new meeting place when we weren't in school.

When we got back to the house I told Mrs. Harris what a wonderful time I had today and that the lunch was great and how it was a pleasure for me to meet her. She replied by saying, "Thank you, Lemmel, and it was also my pleasure to meet you. I look forward to your next visit." I said goodbye to Meagan and Mrs. Harris and started my two mile walk back to the place where I was staying. Meagan and I decided to meet early in the mornings at the library several times a week for the rest of the semester, and make plans for me to come over and visit her at Mrs. Harris place, but something would always happen that kept me away and I couldn't seem to make it over there.

When school was getting close to the end of the semester and my class demands had decreased, there was nothing to interfere from going to visit my lady friend on the weekend. So the first week of May we made plans at the library for me to come over early Saturday morning and we could spend all day together. It was warm enough now, that we could take a swim in the pond. I knew Meagan always had a lot to talk about, and I was looking forward to listening to her and spend a lot of time swimming in the pond. By this time, we had become very close, but we were careful enough that only Mrs. Harris knew that we cared for each other. Saturday finally came. I was going to spend the whole day at the pond with the young woman I had fallen in love with, and she seemed to be just as eager as I was.

Meagan had prepared a big basket lunch for us so there was no need for us to run back up to the house for anything. When we got there, we put down a blanket and Meagan took off her shoes. We just sat for the longest under the trees, talking about the things we were going to do once we finished school. I decided to go for a swim, so I pulled off the pants that I wore over my swimming trunks. I helped Meagan up and we headed for the water. I knew Meagan didn't know how to swim, and she was really reluctant to get in the water. She waded in but stood there just a shivering and moving like a new born calf. She said, "Lemmel! Stop laughing at me because if you don't I am going to go back and sit back down by those trees and let you have this pond to yourself." I said, "Okay, Okay! I want laugh. It's just kind of funny to me to see someone like yourself acting so afraid of water."

Then she asked me "Lemmel what do you mean by that?" "Well you know most of the white people I know can already swim." "I am sorry Lemmel, you are just going to have to be a little patient with me, but you can bet that when I do get in that water, I'm gonna out swim you!" I laughed, took a big breath and dove under the water and didn't surface until I heard her frantically calling my name. I swam over close to her and popped up suddenly in front of her and we laughed and carried on like we were at some comedy show. I did this over and over and then, without warning Meagan started to wade out to the deeper part of the pond and before she knew it the water was up to her shoulders and she started to panic struggling trying to get back to the shallow part. I was watching her from several feet away to see if she would make it back okay when all of a sudden she lost her footing and went under, I almost panicked myself when it happened, but I managed to get to her in a split second. I dove under, grabbed her around the waist and got her head above the water and waded back to the bank.

As I was taking her back I discovered she was hanging on to me for dear life. I had never held a woman like this and I couldn't help but wish that somehow this could go on forever. Of course, her clothes were soaking wet and though it was still late morning, there would be time for the clothes to dry and they would dry faster if I built a fire. While I built a fire, Meagan undressed behind some bushes and dressed in my pants and t-shirt. Trying not to see the way my t-shirt fit her so provocatively and clung to her body, I busied myself helping her to spread her clothes on the nearby bushes. I kept trying not to look, but I began to have feelings I had never experienced before. I became paranoid and nervous because of the guilt I had for thinking the way I was.

To make a long story short Meagan and I made love that very morning, and after that, we couldn't stay away from each other. We were spending more and more time at the pond. Now that we were a few days away from graduation we planned this last Saturday to be together at the pond. So when I made it to Mrs. Harris house just like I normally do I noticed that Mrs.

Harris didn't have that usual smile she always had before when I came by to see Meagan. Meagan didn't even let me come in and sit down before she quickly said goodbye to Mrs. Harris and quickly took me by the hand and headed off to the pond. I asked Meagan did Mrs. Harris feel alright. She said, she's fine, as far as I know and then she asked me why I was asking about Mrs. Harris. I told Meagan that she didn't seem to be the happy person that I had gotten to know. Then she told me, "Lemmel, I have got to tell you something that is very important." My curiosity rose when she told me that, I asked her "What is it, Meagan? What is it?" She said, "Wait 'til we get to the pond! I will tell you when we make it down by the pond."

When we made it down to the pond and spread the blanket, we made tender love for what would be the last time. After taking a short nap I asked her, "When are you planning on telling me your important news?" She looked at me with tears in her eyes and said, "Lemmel, I'm pregnant."

"What! How do you know? Are you sure?" Was all I could say. She began to cry and said, "Yes, I'm sure … I'm pregnant with your baby." "Meagan, stop crying, everything is going to be alright." I held her until she stopped sobbing and said, "Let's think about what we need to do."

I knew that Meagan couldn't take me back to her home in East Texas and tell her parents that I, a Negro, was the father of her baby, and I knew we had to keep this a secret from everyone including Mrs. Harris.

"Why can't we get married and move up north. No one needs to know except us." She was wiping her eyes and laughing at the same time. When I saw she was cheering up, she said, "Lemmel, I would like to keep this just between you and me, but Mrs. Harris already knows about the baby." I asked her, "Well, how could she know this quick?" "Lemmel, she's older and seen a lot more and she could tell before I did because for the last few days I'd been skipping my breakfast because of nausea and taking more naps than I usually do."

I could hear voices coming through the trees but I couldn't see who it was. I turned and asked Meagan if she knew who they were? She said that they were some of her college friends she had invited to come out to the pond. I counted six students coming straight toward us three boys and three girls. I said, "Good grief, Meagan! What are we going to tell them?" She grinned at me, saying, "Lemmel, they already know about you and me, but they know nothing about the baby." So when the students got close enough, they said hello to both of us, chatting away like they'd known us for years. I laid back on the blanket after we pulled it into the sun, and closed my eyes. After a few minutes of listening to their laughter and splashing, I dozed off to sleep when all of a sudden I was awakened by screaming!

One of Meagan's friends had gone under and hadn't come back up! We ran down to the bank where everyone was standing and I noticed that all the boys were accounted for but that there was one girl missing and Meagan immediately knew who was missing. She started screaming for me to do something but I didn't know where to look so the other girls showed me where the girl went under so I dove in immediately and the boys and I searched for the girl for over an hour. She'd been under too long and we all knew that the young lady had drowned. We stopped to rest and someone said we needed the sheriff. One of the older boys was trying to pull up his pants and put his shoes on at the same time to go for help and I was trying to convince Meagan to go back to the house, but she insisted on staying.

I told Meagan that I was going back to tell Mrs. Harris what had happened. She said, "Hurry, and come straight back here!" I said, "Don't worry; I'll be back in no time." When I got back, Meagan came over and grabbed me and just started hugging me and sobbing like she wasn't going to make it. I tried hard to reassure her that everything was going to be alright, but I knew with everything that was happening in her life that this could be the final straw before becoming seriously ill.

The men and women from the city finally made it down to the pond and they searched and searched until it was almost dark, then one of the parents suddenly alarmed everyone that he had found something that was barely in the water but it had the shape of a human body. It turned out to be the girl. She had gotten tangled up in some rope that someone had thrown in the pond and drowned right there near the bank. Mrs. Harris waited for us to come home and when we walked in the house she asked me to have a seat. "I've had several visitors come by here, asking about you two. I told them that you all were just good friends but I don't think they believed me. So this is what we are going to do. Lemmel, I know this is going to be hard for you to do but you are going to have to drop out of school, completely and not come back around here until Meagan has made it back to Kilgore, Texas" Then she told Meagan, "Meagan, you are going to have to be strong until this thing can settle down some." I told Meagan and Mrs. Harris that I just couldn't believe how my day started out so bright and beautiful and now it has come to this. I said,

I'm sorry, Mrs. Harris but I have got to see my Meagan I don't care what I have to do because I don't think I can make it without her." Mrs. Harris said, "Listen to me, Lemmel. I know Meagan has told you about my life in Savannah, Georgia and how I didn't want to leave my son but I had to because it was best for him and my mother, whom I loved dearly." I then asked Meagan how she felt about it she said," Lemmel, I can't answer to anything right now I just want to go and lay down.

CHAPTER

7

Lemmel Travels to Longview Texas In Search Of Meagan

I had gone a whole week without talking to Meagan or Mrs. Harris and it was now after graduation, I wondered what the campus was like since most of the students and professors had left for the summer. I had taken Mrs. Harris' advice and stayed away from the school and her house until everything had cooled off, but now it had started to get to me not knowing how Meagan was doing and whether or not she even was able to graduate from college. It was on a Sunday now when all this was going through my mind so I decided to pay Mrs. Harris a visit early Monday morning and check on her as well as Meagan.

So Monday came and I walked to Mrs. Harris' place. It took close to two hours to get there because I had relocated and found some colored people to stay with since I was no longer going to attend the college. When I made it almost to her house it was still dark but I could see a light on in the house and I knew then that she was probably already up for the day. I found me a place to sit down outside and waited for the sun to rise because I didn't want to knock on her door and she wouldn't be able to see who I was because of the dark.

After about 30 minutes waiting on the sun to come up I got up and went and knocked on her door and to my surprise Meagan answered the door. She pulled the screen door open and without saying a word she was in my arms. We held each other as though we had found our long lost child. After we had hugged for a few minutes she said, "Lemmel, what are you doing coming over here," and I responded by saying, "Meagan, what are you doing still up here in the Chicago area." Then she said, "Lemmel, I don't want to leave without you." When she told me this I knew I would do anything to keep her by my side even if it meant risking my life. Then I asked her what Mrs. Harris thought about it. She said Mrs. Harris was all for us being together, but we have got to be careful and keep control of our emotions and feelings when we are in public. I asked her if she thought I was still welcome over here at Mrs. Harris' house. She laughed and said, "Don't be silly, of course you are, in fact, Mrs. Harris had been up to the school trying to find out where you might be." Meagan and I were still in the front room but I could hear Mrs. Harris stirring around in the kitchen. Mrs. Harris then yelled from the kitchen asking Meagan was there someone at the door. Meagan said loudly, "It's Lemmel Walters! It's Lemmel!" and Mrs. Harris came hurrying into the room, quickly closing the door, and gave me a big hug.

She said to me "Lemmel How have you been, Meagan and I have been worrying ourselves sick wondering what had become of you."

I responded, "Mrs. Harris, there is no need for you all to worry about me because I am from this Chicago area and I know how to take care of myself, but it really makes me feel good to know that I have got wonderful people like you and Meagan thinking about my safety and well-being." Mrs. Harris told me to have a seat and breakfast was going to be ready in just a few more minutes. I said, "Okay because after the 5 mile walk to her house I was ready for something to eat." Meagan had gone to the back for something but after a few minutes she came back and told me to come on and wash up because breakfast is just about ready. After the three of us finished eating, I told Meagan I wanted to help with the dishes, but Mrs. Harris quickly said thanks, but there were more important things for Meagan and me to do. We needed to go back into the living room and sit down and figure out our future. In the meantime the dishes will get done. We said, "Okay, Mrs. Harris, that's what we'll do," then she said, "Come on Lemmel, let's go get started on planning our future."

When we got back up to the front room and sat down I asked Meagan did everything go alright with the graduation she said, "Yes, Lemmel, it was wonderful. I was just wishing you could have been there." She said, "What about you Lemmel? What did your parents say when you told them that you were taking your last few hours of study at the Negro section of the college?" I said "I never did write home and tell them because I don't want my parents worrying about me. Meagan, I have to ask you when are you planning on going home and let your parents know what has been going on in your life." "Lemmel, I plan to go back home in June because I want to be home to help celebrate my parent's 25th wedding anniversary which will be on the 16th of June." "Well, when do you plan on telling them about me and our baby?" "I don't really know, Lemmel. I might not tell them at all because I plan to leave and come back here as soon as the celebration is over." Then I told Meagan that I thought that was a splendid idea but how was the trip going to be financed I asked her. She looked at me and said, "Lemmel, I'm not sure, but I will find a way to get back up here to you. After we had talked for a little while, Mrs. Harris came in and sat down and began talking to us about our situation. A situation neither of us knew how to handle. Mrs. Harris told me that she knew about Meagan's plans to go home and come back without telling her parents, and that she was in full support of Meagan's plan Then I asked Mrs. Harris "What are we going to do about the financing her train ticket." Mrs. Harris told both of us not to worry about the train ticket because she had enough money to buy her a ticket if she wants the money to buy it. Then Meagan leaped to her feet and walked over to where Mrs. Harris was and gave her a big hug and said, "Thank you, thank you! I will work and pay you back every penny." I was so happy I told them both that things are really starting to turn around for us. I think we are going to make it. Meagan turned around and looked at me and said, "Lemmel, if it's a boy I am going to name him Lemmel." I couldn't help but smile and think to myself I am getting ready to become a father. I asked Meagan "Do you think you will be showing by the time you get to Kilgore."

Mrs. Harris reassured us both saying not to worry about that because Meagan, being as tall as she is she won't start showing until she is at least 6 months or more along in the pregnancy. This is when Meagan told me she hadn't gone home yet because she was giving her body time to adjust to the changing of her body. Mrs. Harris told us that Meagan should be ready to travel as soon as Wednesday and that will be the next time there will be a train leaving out for Dallas and Ft. Worth, Texas. I asked her did she feel like she would be ready by Wednesday. She said, "Oh yes, Lemmel! In fact I already feel well enough to travel but Mrs. Harris thinks I should wait a couple of more days." "Well, ladies, I guess I'll start making plans to let my parents know what's going on." "Mrs. Harris said, "Yes, Lemmel, I think that would be a good idea because I think that you are a fine young man and if they knew how much you have been through they would be very proud of you." Then I said, "Thank you, Mrs. Harris, that's really nice of you to say that! Now what time is the train scheduled to leave on Wednesday?" "7:30 a.m., "Meagan said. Then Mrs. Harris said, "Lemmel, I know that it may be a little hard on the both of you but you shouldn't come see Meagan off down at the train station." "No, Mrs. Harris, I didn't plan on coming down to the station.

I thought I could come back here to the house and see her off from here." "Good," Meagan said, "I think that is an excellent idea, Lemmel." I had to bring my visit to an end because I knew Meagan and I would have talked and visited all day and I had to be strong for the both of us. So I told them I would see them Wednesday morning early and I set out on the long walk back to my rooms. I promised Mrs. Harris that I was going to let my parents know, and I meant to, but all I had on my mind, was Meagan and how much I loved her and the sorrow I felt that we had to be secretive.

Wednesday came and the little time I had with Meagan went by so fast it seemed like something I might have dreamed. By Friday, midday, I was missing Meagan so bad I couldn't eat. It seemed like it was only yesterday that we were at the pond having a good time, not worrying about anything in the world.

Since she had been gone, I was adrift, without a rudder. I knew my only hope was to go over to Mrs. Harris' house and hopefully find some kind of comfort there. So I headed over to Mrs. Harris' to visit with her. It didn't matter, now that Meagan was gone, just who might see me going over there. I just wanted to talk to someone who knew her like I did.

When I walked up on Mrs. Harris' porch to knock she had already seen me from her open window so when she opened the door, I could tell she had been crying by her red eyes. She welcomed me in and of course, offered me a seat. I asked her what might the problem be, and could I help? "Lemmel, there is nothing really wrong. I just miss Meagan and I've been worrying about my baby girl ever since she got on the train Wednesday, I have just had a bad feeling about it."

"What do you think could be the problem? Do you think she might be in danger or something like that? I'd be really appreciative if you gave me a better idea." Then she really broke down and cried even harder and that's when I lost it, we both just cried and cried for several minutes.

When I finally regained my composure, I got up and went over and sat down next to her, put my arms around her and comforted her the best I could. "Mrs. Harris straightened her posture, saying, "I'm alright." I asked her, "What can we do Mrs. Harris." She replied, "No Lemmel, it's what you can and will do." I said, "Tell me what I do, and I I'll try my best to do it." " Mrs. Harris said, "Tomorrow is Saturday. There will be a train leaving at 8 o'clock in the morning heading south. I am going to give you enough money to buy you a round trip ticket to Longview Texas, but that will be as for as you can go so you will have to find you a family to stay with in Longview until after the June 16th anniversary celebration. I have already written this letter to Meagan telling her what the plan will be."

I was so glad I had decided to visit her today because I had no idea that she would supply me with the money I needed to go see about my Meagan. She said she thought it would be best if I went home and packed and came back prepared to spend the night. So without asking any questions I left and did exactly what she told me to do. Saturday morning, Mrs. Harris served me biscuits and gravy and packed me some biscuits and ham for the trip. As I was traveling on the train headed to Texas I noticed that the farther south I got, the more I would see Negro train conductors and porters working the trains. Since Meagan had left, I hadn't slept well nor had much of an appetite, and I knew I needed to get some sleep. So after we stopped in Missouri and headed for Texas I made it a point to go to sleep and keep sleeping as long as I could. After a few days the train pulled into Longview, and the porters offered help with my luggage, I declined. I did ask if they knew of a place to stay that was cheap and clean.

There was a Negro porter working the trains that reminded me a lot of Roosevelt. He told me to look up Professor Samuel Jones and Dr. Calvin Davis, that one of them they could surely help me out. Dr. Davis lived about a mile west of the train station, just off Nelson Street and I got there in no time, due to the accuracy of the direction. He offered me a cold glass of tea and we just seemed to hit it off immediately. I was only there a few minutes, and someone knocked on the door. It was Professor Jones. Dr. Davis informed me that he had an extra room that I could use while I was in town. I thanked him and told him I was happy to accept his invitation. As the three of us were riding back to Professor Jones house, Dr. Davis asked me, "Lemmel, what are your plans now since you have made it all the way to Longview from Chicago?"

I told him that I had just finished up most of my studies in the dentistry field and was looking for an opportunity to start a practice somewhere in Texas; it would really be beneficial to me learning my craft as a professional dentist. Dr. Davis then told me, "Lemmel, I think that is great you being a young dentist just starting out and me already having a good practice here in Longview, this could be the beginning of a good thing for the two of us." Since I was from a large city like Chicago, and looking around at Longview, I really wasn't convinced that there would be a lot of business in Longview but once he told me about all the potential business that was in Gregg County I actually started to become a little excited about the fact that I could have a good life here. I told Dr. Davis, "Thank you! I think that this will be really good for me to have the opportunity to work under an already established dentist."

As Dr. Davis was pulling up to Professor Jones' house and let him out of the car he was driving but then it dawned on me that I really wouldn't be able to take my practice serious here because my soul purpose and my only purpose was to stay in Longview just long enough to take Meagan back to Chicago. When we got back to Dr. Davis' and went inside, his wife Julia was coming from the kitchen. She didn't seem to be any older than 18, but I knew that both she and Dr. Davis were in their late twenties or early thirties. He told her my plans and said he wanted her consent for me to stay at the house for a while. She was exuberant, and exclaimed that she would be delighted for me to stay. Dr. Davis could certainly use a dentist friend to talk business with and she could use some of that time for herself, she remarked with a twinkle in her eye. She said that the extra bedroom was just going to waste. I realized it was getting close to about six in the evening and Mrs. Davis already had supper ready to serve. She prepared a plate for me as though she had known I was coming to dinner.

During dinner, Dr. Davis informed me he has riding horses, and invited me to see them after dinner. We walked outside to his stables and I was surprised at the beautiful animals he had. I told Dr. Davis that, "These are some of the finest horses I have ever seen, in fact these animals are a whole lot better looking than all the ones I've seen back home In Chicago." Then he asked if I rode and I replied that I did. "Lemmel, you and I will go riding Sunday after church and I will show you some of the country side." I thought to myself that this was perfect because it would allow me to get some what oriented in Gregg County.

CHAPTER

8

Lemmel Will Go To His First Negro Business League Meeting

When Sunday morning came we attended church he and his wife and I, and he introduced me to all of his church members, I thought to myself that I had never been around so many people that were so friendly, and it seemed that they were truly genuine in offering me a place to stay, and even the parents were making it a point to introduce their unattached daughters to me. But I was keeping everything to myself because all

I had on my mind was Meagan and how soon I would be able to see her and hold her in my arms.

When we made it back to Dr. Davis' home, he told me I had plenty of time to change clothes and relax because it was going to be a little later before we got the horses out. Julia served dinner and we had a really nice conversation about the little towns near Longview. I had to pretend that I didn't know anything about Kilgore, and he told me it was a part of Gregg County and only about 10 miles from Longview. I can drive it in about 30 minutes, but it would take a lot longer on horseback. Then I asked him, "Dr. Davis, where exactly, are we going to be riding to today?" "Well, Lemmel I was thinking about riding down to Camp Switch and on the way you would get a chance to meet a lot of the Negro families that are living in that area." I was hoping he would say Kilgore but I knew that I had to play it smart and pretend that I was excited about riding down to Camp Switch with him. Dr. Davis said that the reason he rode later in the day was because he didn't want the horses to get overheated riding them in the heat of the day, and the other reason was because of the racism in East Texas that seemed to be at a fever pitch these days. I asked him, "Why do you think the tension is so great in this country?"

He said, "It's just the way society is right now. If you are a Negro the white man believes by you being a Negro, you should stay in your place." "What exactly do you mean, Dr. Davis, when you say the white man believes we should stay in our place?" "Let me give you an example. Let's just say you were a black man and you had several acres of land that you and your family had worked and it was yielding a nice crop of cotton. Do you know that the white cotton growers feel like they should be the ones who should make the decisions concerning your cotton?

Now, I mean the very cotton you and your family planted and picked." This whole thing about racism being at an all-time high was really starting to bother me because I was deeply in love with a white woman from the south and she was just as in love with me. I asked him if he thought that maybe money was the main thing that the white man wants to control. He looked at me pausing for a second and said, "Sure, Lemmel, that's one of the main things, but if he thought a Negro man was getting too close to his daughter or sister you would see in him a man that you've never seen before."

The entire time I spent this Sunday with Dr. and Mrs. Davis, my mind was on one thing and that was how I was going to find Meagan and get her back to Chicago. As we were sitting around one late afternoon, I asked Dr. Davis, what his hobby was when he wasn't practicing medicine. "You know, Lemmel I'm glad you asked me that because there are a lot of things I'm involved in right now and one of the main things is the unfair treatment of the Negro by the white merchants or the cotton brokers in this area." Then I asked him, "Are you one of the leaders of the NAACP." He said, "Yes, I am because the NAACP can't babysit every Negro businessman in his dealings with those in this society who will never deal with him on an equal basis.

This is why Professor Jones and I have found it necessary to establish the Negro Business League for the farmers and cotton growers in Gregg County." I was starting to become very interested and curious as to how the Negro Businesses League operated here in Gregg County. So I asked him," Just exactly how did it work for the people and what was its function."

"Well, Lemmel," he said, "you know Longview is not my home but my wife and I have lived here for the past several years now, and we have witnessed a lot of Negro families moving away because of the oppression they suffered from the white society, so I decided to get involved with the farmers and especially the cotton growers that will be selling their cotton this September and October. You know, when we moved to Longview from Marshall in the year 1909, it seemed that over half of the families living here were Negro families and it seemed to be the place to be if you were a Negro, but as the years passed, especially the last couple of years, most of the farmers have been leaving this area searching for a better place to call home." I really started to feel like I had a better understanding of what it was like to live in East Texas.

I asked him, "Dr. Davis, do you have many members in the Negro Businessmen League." He said,

"Yes, in fact, we have one of our weekly meetings tomorrow night down at Camp Switch, and then on Thursday night there will be another one held down by the Sabine River for the Negro farmers living in the community of Easton and Mayflower, Elderville , and Harris Chapel. "Dr. Davis, I asked him, "How far are these communities located from Kilgore?" "I don't know exactly, Lemmel, but Elderville in going to be the closest one of them to Kilgore." He thought for a moment, looking at me. Finally, he said, "You've mentioned Kilgore a few times now, so I get the impression that Kilgore or something in Kilgore is of great interest to you." "Trying to act nonchalant, I said, "Don't you think if we could get the Negro businessmen in the Kilgore area to join the league, the numbers would make it a lot stronger?"

Then he looked over at Mrs. Davis and said, "This young man is far beyond his years in the way he thinks." I was thinking to myself that Dr. Davis just didn't know just how far I was in a forbidden interracial relationship with a young white lady living in Kilgore. Mrs. Davis suggested to Dr. Davis that he go and get the horses out because she didn't want us to be on the road too late at night.

Dr. Davis motioned for me to come outside with him and saddle up the horses for the evening ride that we were going to take. When we got out back I could see the horses a little ways off, standing under some trees that were in the pasture. Dr. Davis led the way into the barn and showed me the tack room where he kept the saddles and bridles. We walked out of the back of the barn, and Dr. Davis started yelling, "Red! Red! Come here, boy!" That's when this horse started running our direction at a full gallop. I looked to see another horse, a pretty grey, topping the rise headed in our direction. I didn't say anything to Dr. Davis but I figured that his horse Red must be the one in front of the other one.

When the two horses finally made it up to where we were I could see that Red looked to stand about 17 hands high and maybe weighed about 1200 pounds or more, he had a solid red coat. The other horse wasn't quite as large as Red, but his eyes showed great intelligence. Red was a stud, but the grey was a gelding. I asked Dr. Davis the grey's name and he said Doc. "I named him Doc because I bought him when he was just a colt several years ago and to make a long story short he is the first horse I rode to make my rounds when I started practicing medicine here in the Longview area."

Once we got the horses all saddled up and were ready to ride, we mounted up and headed for Camp Switch. Dr. Davis was leading the way when all of sudden he stopped and turned around and headed back toward the house. Then he headed off on a trail away from the main road. As we rode along, he mentioned there had been a lot of really bad things happening in Longview since the war had come to an end, and our Negro soldiers coming home. There has been a lot of old time slavery talk being spread by some of the most prominent white people in this Longview area. I asked him what he meant by "old time slavery" talk. He went on to tell me that it was all in the way the whites address me now, opposed to how they addressed me when I first came here from Marshall back in 1909. "They used to call me Dr. Davis

but now they just call me Davis Boy or just plan Boy."
I asked him, "Dr. Davis, do they ever threaten the
Negroes around here with physical harm?"

He said, "Yes, they have, Lemmel, but I won't
talk about that right now, they're not empty threats,
but are to be taken seriously. We'll talk about that
later. I don't want to scare you on your first horseback
ride in East Texas." He told me as we were riding
along the trail that we are going to stay on this trail
until we made it out of Longview, and then we are
going to ride alongside the railroad tracks the rest of
the way to Camp Switch. I noticed as we were riding
that there were acres and acres of land planted in
nothing but cotton stretching as far as the eye could
see. I asked Dr. Davis, who owned of all these cotton
fields.

"Well Lemmel," he said, pausing, for a second,
"The railroad track is a divider between the white
folk's land and the Negro property, and that one of his
closest white friends owned or shared in most of the
cotton fields in Gregg County." We had been riding for
almost 30 minutes now and still all I saw were cotton

fields, so I asked Dr. Davis who he thought was going to make the most money from the cotton this year, the Negro farmer or the white farmer? "Since Professor Jones and I established and organized the Negro Businessmen's League a few years ago, a lot of the cotton money has been coming back to the Negro cotton growers and this year looks to be a prosperous one for all growers."

I figured if the Negroes were becoming more prosperous in Gregg County that meant that the white dignitaries were somewhat sympathetic toward the Negro businessman, therefore allowing everyone to make money off of their perspective cotton, but the most important thing it seemed that the whites and Negroes were in harmony with one another. As we were riding up to the Camp Switch station I noticed that there were several cars and trucks park over by a small shed that resembled an old house. I could see the men gathering all around and talking getting ready for the meeting.

As we neared the meeting barn, two young Negro men came and took the horses away tying them to one of the nearby trees that were located around the back of the barn. There were several white men approached Dr. Davis, greeting him with a handshake and introducing themselves to me. I was beginning to feel like I was someone important already, and I didn't really know what the meeting was going to be all about. It was starting to get close to 7:30pm when Dr. Davis told everyone to come up to the front of the barn and find somewhere comfortable to sit down. I was thinking that I was the only one burning up from the heat but the Texans were also hot , and Dr. Davis was going to have the meeting right outside under the shade trees where it was kind of cool. He started the meeting by taking a head count of those present, thanked everyone for coming out and especially Mr. Jones and Mr. Sims, the two white men who were members of the Negro Businessmen League.

I could tell that the two white men were very important members because he asked them to stand and come on up to the front where he was and explain to the other members about the rising and falling of the cotton bales prices and to be aware of the growth in Gregg County and all the timber that is being sold in this county alone. After about35 minutes of answering questions from the members, without any warning, Dr. Davis called me up to the front and introduced me to all the members. He gave the impression that I was a new member and that I was going to be the one to help with the changes or for the better treatment of the Negro people living in Gregg County. I said hello to everyone and that I enjoyed listening to the questioning and answering session here this evening.

Then for some reason I began to feel guilty about my real reason for coming to Texas in the first place. It seemed to me no matter what was happening or where I was, I just couldn't get Meagan off my mind. The meeting had come to a close when Dr. Davis asked everyone to bow their heads for a word of prayer, and after the prayer, a lot of hand shaking, everyone began to leave. Dr. Davis made sure everyone left safely, so this would cause us to be the last ones to leave. Now that we were on our way back home, he said to me that we could go a deferent way back and that we would travel the dirt roads instead of the trails used the first time. It didn't take nearly as long to get back to Longview as it did for us to get to Camp Switch. When we got back to Dr. Davis' neighborhood he told me that we were going to stop over at his father-in- law's house and visit with him for a few minutes. I said, "That will be fine, Dr. Davis, it's still a little early."

When we made it up to the house we got down off the horses and with him leading the way knocked on the door for his father-in-law to answer. Someone from inside asked, "Who is it!" Dr. Davis replied, "It's Cal and a new doctor that has come to town." He opened the door and said, "C'mon in son, and you too young man, I would offer you all something to eat but since my wife has been ill, I only cook enough food for 2 and whatever is left I have to throw it out, I am sorry."

"That's okay dad. We were just stopping by for a few minutes before we headed on down to the house with the horses." "Has something happened again Cal," he asked with a certain chill in his voice. Dr.

Davis looked over to where I was standing, but I pretended to be looking outside keeping a check on the horses. He said, "No dad, we had a meeting tonight down at Camp Switch with some of the members of the Negro Businessmen's League, so we stopped by your place to visit with you for a while and let the horses cool off before going on home, and I wanted to make sure Mama is alright and see if she needs anything."

Then he suggested that we all have a seat and just relax for a few minutes. So we sat down, and Dr. Davis introduced Mr. Bush as his father-in-law and me to Mr. Bush as young Dr. Lemmel Walters, a young man who has come all the way from Chicago, Illinois to begin his dentistry right here in Gregg County. Mr. Bush looked at me and started nodding his head as to say congratulations. I still didn't have very much to say about it because I hadn't completed all of my training necessary to be a doctor, and my main reason for coming to Longview was to get to Kilgore and find a young white woman in this land named Meagan Reese. Mr. Bush asked me was I thinking about becoming a member of the League. I said, "Mr. Bush, I attended my first meeting today and I really enjoyed it because I found it to be very informative for the Negroes living in this area and yes, you can certainly consider me to be a member of the League." Dr. Davis said, "Lemmel, this is wonderful, a young man like yourself taking an interest in today's affairs even though you have gotten an education for yourself." Our visit was concluded shortly after, so Mr. Bush walked us outside where we remounted the horses and he waved us off.

As we were riding back to Dr. Davis house I could barely see his horse because of the dark, I also noticed that while we were passing by Professor Jones place I could see a dull faint light glowing from the front window of his house. Dr. Davis could sense that I was becoming a little nervous riding in the dark the way we were, so he asked me, "Lemmel, what are you thinking about." I said, "Dr. Davis, I'm from the city of Chicago and it is going to take a little getting used to for me riding in the dark like this," but that wasn't what my mind was really on, and I still couldn't help but think about the question that Mr. Bush had asked Dr. Davis when he said to him has something else happened. That aroused my curiosity even more because of the way in which Dr. Davis had traveled to Camp Switch one way and come back another way. Dr. Davis let me know that East Texas wasn't all that far behind the rest of the states. Marshall, Texas, to be more specific was the first town in Texas to have electricity and lights even though the Negro part of town was still without electricity.

As we approached Dr. Davis home I could see that all the lights were on, so it seemed to me, but when we got inside the house there were only two lights on and they were the front light and the kitchen light. Mrs. Davis seemed to be really glad to see us coming in, and she said to Dr. Davis and me, "Cal and Lemmel, I've got plenty of food prepared for you all in the kitchen, so wash up and we'll all eat dinner before turning in for the night."

While we were sitting at the dinner table I asked Dr. Davis what his itinerary looked like for the week. He looked at me smiling, almost laughing it seemed, then he replied and said "Lemmel, I don't like to brag or sound boastful but I am a self-made man because of the education I received in Marshall, Texas at the Negro college and now I'm putting it to use by serving the Negro community as a doctor and as one of the leaders of equality for the Negroes living in Gregg County, but to answer your question, I'll be taking off tomorrow, and Tuesday I will travel to the Kilgore area so I will have the rest of the week to concentrate on my clients that are here in Longview."

Then I asked him, "Do you think I will have a chance to meet some of the people that are living in Longview." "Why, I am pretty sure you will because I am going to fill up my 1915 ford with plenty of gas and you and Professor Jones will be with me all day tomorrow traveling through the community gathering the latest news for the local newspaper Professor Jones has started publishing. " Monday everything went exactly the way Dr. Davis said it would, and we were back home eating supper with Mrs. Davis before dark. During dinner, Dr. Davis told me to get plenty of sleep because tomorrow was going to be a busy day for us. So on this particular night I would have time to write Mrs. Harris a letter letting her know that I had made it to Texas and that everything was fine with the Negro family I was staying with in Longview. I went to bed early so I would be ready to rise early that morning and travel to the Kilgore area with Dr. Davis.

The next morning came just as quickly as I had closed my eyes it seemed. After we had finished breakfast, Dr. Davis and I went into his office that was attached to his house and took out his medical bag, doctor tools and medicine so we could load them in his car.

When we got everything loaded and ready to go we looked in the back seat of the car and there sat Calvin Jr. all set and ready to go. Dr. Davis began laughing at the lad but Calvin Jr. seemed very serious about going with his dad this morning.

Dr. Davis, laughingly asked, Jr., just where do you think you are going?" Jr. quickly responded, "I am going with you, dad" Then Dr. Davis went over to him and placed his hand on top of his head and began telling him just how much his mother Julia and his little sister Vivian needed him to stay home and protect them until he could make it back home later on that evening. The explanation that Dr. Davis gave him went over really well it seemed, because Jr., being only 3 years got right out of the vehicle without trading words and went back into the house with a look of responsibility on his face. Then Dr. Davis shaking his head turned to me and asked me was I ready to go? I said to him, "I'm ready whenever you are." So he made a quick trip to the house to say goodbye to his wife and his children. Now that everything was settled at home Dr. Davis and I were finally off to pick up Professor Jones and head to Kilgore. When we made it to Professor Jones' house, I got out of the car in order for the Professor to have his choice on whether he wanted the back seat or the front seat. He chose the back seat. I didn't show it but I was so glad to be sitting in the front because this would give me a chance to view the country side and hopefully I would be able to locate the white family home.

After we picked up the Professor, Dr. Davis pulled out of his drive way and headed down a dirt road heading south to Kilgore, as we were traveling on the dirt road I noticed that the rail road tracks were laid almost exactly along the road that we were traveling. I asked Dr. Davis where the tracks led. He said, "Lemmel, these tracks run all the way to Kilgore and on to Palestine Texas, about 95 miles to the south."

After we had traveled for a couple of miles the train tracks were no longer visible and Dr. Davis would make one of several stops delivering the medicine to some of his clients. When we all got back in his car he told Professor Jones and me that he was going to cut back and get on the main road to Kilgore. By me being in the front I could see everything that was coming up in including the river that we were approaching, I didn't know how far we were going to have to ride before we cross the river but I figured that it wouldn't be too far away since we had already made it to the main road to Kilgore. After we had traveled a short distance Dr. Davis slowed down the car in order to cross safely over the wooden bridge. Once we had made it over to the other side I couldn't see anything but fields and fields of cotton and people working in the fields or chopping cotton like locust, it looked like some of the babies were even chopping cotton. I said to myself that this was truly the land of cotton.

CHAPTER

9

Lemmel Will Catch Up With Meagan at Her Home in Kilgore, Texas

Even though it seemed that we had done a lot that morning but it wasn't 8:00 yet and we had already stopped at some of Dr. Davis clients homes and were now entering the Kilgore city limits. I knew that Dr. Davis was going to go to the Negro neighborhood and take care of his patients over there, but I still found myself asking him about the white citizens in Kilgore and did he practice medicine in the white neighborhood.

He said, "No, Lemmel, I don't practice over there at all. Any patients that I do have over in the white neighborhood are the Negroes that still live close to the white folks that they work for." After a couple of hours in the Negro neighborhood we headed to the white side of town to check on the Negro patients that were live in helpers at a couple of the white's homes. When we got over to one of the homes it seemed that an entire Negros family was living with their employers because of the number of children that came out to greet us when we drove up. For some reason I still felt guilty for being so deceptive in my motives for asking Dr. Davis so many questions about Kilgore. I anxiously got out of the car so I could greet the Negroes and start asking questions about the people living there in the neighborhood. I noticed that Professor Jones wasn't very talkative and hadn't spoken 3 words the whole while we'd been together but I could tell that he was very observant and intelligent. I strolled over to one of the teen aged girls that were there and asked her, "Do you know of a Meagan Reese? She replied by saying, "Yes. Everybody around here knows of the Reese family."

I was just about ready to blow my secret when I suddenly realized that this wasn't just about a white lady and me, this was also about an unborn child that hadn't made any of these choices that Meagan and I were going to have to deal with. I asked the young lady where might the Reese place be located and she said right up the street about a half of a mile. And they've got several small shacks for the Negro employees to live in while the cotton is being chopped. I thought to myself that this is too good to be true.

I was so excited and elated about the possibility of seeing Meagan I could no longer carry on a conversation with the young lady, so I went and sat in the car to wait for Dr. Davis to finish up with his patients so we could move on down the street to the Reese place. I knew that Professor Jones had heard me asking questions about Meagan but I didn't really care at that time because I was finally getting close to seeing her for the first time since she had left Chicago.

As Professor Jones and I were sitting in the car waiting on Dr. Davis to take us on down to the Reese place we didn't say a word to one another. As we pulled up to the large house with giant columns just like some of the old plantation houses I had seen, I could see the small shacks that lined up at the edge of the fields looking like they grew up and sprouted up with the cotton plants. There would be trails for the car to travel up to the shacks but we had to pass by the big house first before we could get to them. Dr. Davis stopped and checked with the Reese's to see if any of their spring employees needed his services, but for some reason the house looked as though it was deserted. So we got out of the car and Dr. Davis went up and knocked on the front door and no one answered, so I went around to the back of the house to see if anyone was home, and lo and behold! There stood Meagan looking like something beautiful that had been cut out of a catalog. I stopped in my tracks when I saw her and she seemed to freeze as well, then all at once, she screamed, "Lemmel! Lemmel! What are you doing here," and ran into my arms and we were kissing and hugging, totally oblivious to anyone who might be around.

Again I knew I was playing it close but at the moment, holding Meagan in my arms was all I could dream of and I didn't care what happened to me because she and the baby were all that was on my mind. I asked her, "Meagan, where is everyone." She said, "Lemmel, you won't believe this but everyone has gone down town to pick up the supplies for this week and I stayed home with the helpers we have in our cotton fields." I asked her how long it would be before they got back and she said they'd be gone for at least another two hours. I was thinking that this would give me plenty of time to spend with my girl, Meagan. I said, "Come on to the front where Dr. Davis is. He's come by to check with you to see if there will be any need for his services today. When we got back round front to where Dr. Davis was, she introduced herself and said a proper hello. She told Dr. Davis there was a young man that was staying in shack number 3 that had a bad cut on his leg and there was a good chance he would need some stitches. Dr. Davis said to me,

"Lemmel, do you think you are ready to sew up a human leg." I would deceive him once again by saying no. I don't think I am ready yet. My mind was on how much time Meagan and I had together before Dr. Davis would finish up his business in Kilgore. So I asked him how long it was going to take him he said around 45minutes if everything went well. Meagan and I wouldn't have minded if he'd said all day, we just wanted to make up for lost time. I said okay and we went back around the house and sat down and began reminiscing about our times back in Chicago. She asked me about Mrs. Harris, I told her, "Mrs. Harris is doing fine but I have to admit that when you first left, she took it very hard."

"Well Lemmel, looking at me and grinning, she asked, "How did you do when I left." I told her, "Meagan, you don't have to ask that question! You can see what it was doing to me and I did something about it." I could tell Megan was very happy with me because she laughed at my every word. Then suddenly it was like the earth was standing still and nothing was moving because reality had set in ... Meagan asked me in an almost whisper, "Lemmel, how did you get all way down here and to my house?" 'Well Meagan that's kind of a long story but I'll try to make it short. Mrs. Harris gave me a round trip ticket to come down here and bring you back to Chicago immediately after your parents' anniversary party is over."

She said "Yes! Yes! Lemmel that would be great! "Well, Meagan, I can see Dr. Davis coming back this way, so everything must have gone well with man who needed stitches." As we stood there she reached over and grabbed me in a big hug, and was kissing me, and I responded by hugging her back.

In the back of my mind, was the thought that I needed to get out of Kilgore for a little while so Meagan and I could cool off. "Megan said, "Lemmel how are we going to see each other again?" I said "I don't know Meagan, but I know where you are now, so I'll be back to see you." When I looked at Meagan, she had tears in her eyes. I said, "What's wrong?" She said, "Nothing is wrong, Lemmel." I thought that she would have been happy, but it seemed that I had made her sad showing up like I did, and now I was leaving her all over again. I was beginning to feel badly about the whole thing, and I said, "Meagan, what do you want me to do? Just say it, I will do it." She said, "Lemmel, I don't want you to go back with Dr. Davis. You could stay right here in one of the shacks and help with the cotton until we can go back to Chicago and get married."

"I don't know anything about cotton!" "Well, it won't matter that much because in a couple of weeks we'll be on our way." I said, "Okay, Meagan, but I'll have to figure out a way to get Dr. Davis to bring me back up here." So as the car came back to pick me up I once again had to say goodbye to part of me. It was now about 11:00 and we were figuring on being back in Longview about 11:30, so we were right on schedule. As we left out of the Kilgore city limits I was just thinking of ways for me to get back over to Meagan's house, and I was now very familiar with the railroad tracks that stretched from Longview to Kilgore because of the route Dr. Davis had taken us. After we had made it a few miles out of town Professor Jones started asking me questions about my relationship with the white lady that was over at the Reese's place. I pretended not to know what he was talking about so I asked him, "What house are you referring to, Professor?" Trying to act as though I was confused, when in fact, I knew exactly what he was talking about. Professor Jones then started telling Dr. Davis what I had asked the Negro girl about the Reese family.

At this point I knew that my secret was no longer a secret. Dr. Davis looked over at me and said, "Lemmel, do you want to tell Professor Jones and me what exactly is going on with you and the white woman living in Kilgore." I felt myself getting a little angry and defensive with Dr. Davis and Professor Jones for the way they were coming at me with all those questions that I was not prepared to answer just yet. But before we got to the Sabine River I had told them the whole story concerning Meagan and me. Professor Jones said, "Lemmel, you seem like a very nice young man so as your father would probably say to you, if you are in love with her and she feels the same way, I strongly advise you not to go back to

Kilgore for any reason. The racial tension is far too great in Gregg County and if her kin find out, they might do something really rash."

Then I couldn't help but to ask both of them, "Is it really that bad? Is there something I need to know?" "Dr. Davis said, "Lemmel, I didn't want to bother you with all the bad secrets that are hidden in Longview and Kilgore by the sheriff's department and the local press, but some of our outspoken Negroes have been coming up missing, especially those soldiers that have come back from the war." "Do you have any idea what may have happened to them, I asked." Professor Jones said, "Oh yes Lemmel, I know exactly what happened to a couple of them because I followed the KKK as they had dragged two Negro veterans from their horses, threw them into cars, and took them out of town. They haven't been heard from since." I asked him, "And you didn't report this to the authorities." "Sometimes it's best to leave some things alone. Dr. Davis and I know of several cases where white men and women have come up missing and we have a good idea that the Negroes are that are behind it." You know something, sir? I'm glad I met you two when I got off of the train. You seem to be at the head of everything and well informed about the affairs of this county. Professor Jones told me that the things he won't print in the Chicago Defender, he will start writing about them in the local Negro newspaper called the Brothers Eyes. It was now about noon when we drove through the Mobberly Edition, which was the Black neighborhood for those Negroes living in Longview. Dr. Davis drove us straight to his home so we could eat lunch.

I didn't have much of an appetite because of all the things I had gone through earlier that morning, especially the visit I had with Meagan. When we walked in the house Mrs. Davis said, "Come on in everyone, you are just in time for a Sunday meal prepared on a week day just for you. I could smell something cooking but I really didn't know what it was but it was making my lost appetite come back to me. I asked Mrs. Davis what was that I smelled because it smelt so good. Dr. Davis and Professor Jones kind of looked at each other and just smiled, shaking their heads as they walked to the kitchen to wash up before eating their lunch. I quickly asked Mrs. Davis, "What are they laughing about?"

She looked at me with a grin half laughing herself, and said, "Lemmel, what you smell is southern fried chicken, a very common dish here in the south, but don't worry. I do realize that you are from Chicago and fried chicken is not prepared up there as much as it is down here." After a delicious meal, Dr. Davis asked Professor Jones and me to come out to his office because he had something to show us. When we walked in to his office he walked over to the plastic cover and pulled it back and there laid two brand new pistols still in the boxes looking like toys but I could tell they were the real thing. I asked Dr. Davis just what he was planning to do with these guns. He said "Lemmel, I call these my two new pet rattlesnakes and whenever I get in a jam with the white people these two pistols are going to help back me up." I was thinking to myself that I hadn't ever been around a man such as Dr. Davis who was so cautious and well prepared for anything that might happen. Dr. Davis picked up one of the guns and a box of bullets and asked us if we were we ready to go. I didn't know where but I said yes.

Dr. Davis told us that there were a lot of cotton fields over at Willow Springs and it was mostly all colored people living in that neighborhood and that's why he decided to take along one of his pets with him. Professor Jones asked him if he was expecting problems over there. "I don't really know Professor Jones. I don't think we are going have any problems but it's like my friend Mayor Bodenheim always says, "Prepare for the worst but hope for the best." I asked Dr. Davis if he was going to Willow Springs to start another business league for the white businessman. He said, "No, Lemmel, there is only one businessmen's league and that's the one you attended a few days ago. I don't want you to get the wrong idea about the league Lemmel; it's for everyone no matter what the color of their skin is."

"Then why are we going there," I asked.

"Well, there's a man that's going to have a good crop of cotton this year and he wants me to come over to his house and show him the different ways that he can sell his cotton bales straight to the brokers in Houston rather than pay a large sum of money to the local brokers in order for them to sell his cotton for him."

Then Professor Jones said, "We've already signed up several white men as members of the Negro businessmen League." Dr. Davis looked over at me and said, "Lemmel, I know what you are thinking but I want you to know that the Negro Businessmen's League was organized by the Negroes but the business concepts can be used by anyone." When we finally drove up to the white man's house, I noticed that he had several Negro men working for him. "Hello. Mr. Wallace," Dr. Davis said cheerfully. "Hey Calvin, how are you doing." Dr. Davis got out of the car he and Mr. Wallace shook hands. I was still trying to get used to all the cotton fields that I was seeing. Professor Jones went out and looked out at all the fields and came back and told Mr. Wallace and Dr. Davis, Now I understand why everyone is saying that the money is in Willow Springs this year." Mr. Wallace laughed and said to Professor Jones, "Why do you say that."

"Because there is more cotton and corn planted out here than I have seen in a long time." Mr. Wallace said, "You know Calvin, it's going to be different this year with the money and all that's made from the crops." I spoke up and said, "Yes I can tell that things are going to be different, but for the Negro farmers it will still be the same unless the Negro Businessmen's League can get involved and help those black cotton pickers out, especially those that you have working for you, Mr. Wallace." "Yes son, you are absolutely correct!

That's why Calvin and Sam are here, to help us with the distributing of profits equally." "Well," Dr. Davis said to Mr. Wallace, "Tell us all about your plans for this coming fall's cotton sales." He replied, "Calvin, most people think that all of that cotton is mine that you see planted out there but in reality it belongs to those black men that are out there chopping it."

Mr. Davis asked him again, "Exactly what is your interest going to be, Mr. Wallace" Mr. Davis, he said, "Those guys and I are going to split the profit 4 ways this time instead of the usual 50% my take and they split the rest." Then, Dr. Davis told Mr. Wallace that he thought that that was a great plan and that he was going to make sure that he and his Negro partners would get the exposure they needed in order to deal with the cotton dealers in Galveston. When Dr. Davis and Mr. Wallace had concluded their meeting, he stood up and stretched for a few seconds, turned to Professor Jones and me and asked us if we were ready to ride. I was the first one to answer and say, yes. Even though it wasn't even late afternoon, I was ready to go home for the night because I still had just one thing on my mind and that was getting Meagan away from Kilgore and back to Chicago and I needed some time to sit and figure out a plan. When we started back toward Longview, Dr. Davis informed Professor Jones and me that he was going to stop by and talk to Mayor Bodenheim to let him know about some of the changes the cotton growers were going to be making this coming fall concerning the cotton brokers in Galveston. I was thinking to myself when he was telling us this that I really didn't know the mayor at all, and I wondered if it was a good idea for the doctor to inform him about anything concerning the Negro Businessmen's League. It seemed to me at times that Dr. Davis could actually read my mind because he would always start telling me about the things I was already thinking about. Dr. Davis said, "Lemmel, I know that you may be wondering why I associate myself with the whites in this county." "Dr. Davis, you're reading my mind."

That's when he glanced over at me and started laughing. "Well, let me try and explain something to you about my relationships with the white people and the county officials that we have around here. No matter how bad the racial tension might be at this time, it's still in the best interest of everyone, especially the Negroes that we try and keep in close contact with the whites because if we don't, we will lose out on a lot of the things in the capital and a great deal in the business world. Even though Gabriel Bodenheim is white and the mayor of Longview and, one of the largest cotton brokers in the United States, I still consider him to be my friend and business associate. Hearing this, I started to feel a lot better about my love affair with Meagan and began to feel like Dr. Davis might be able to have a positive influence on the whole thing. I was relieved it was out and on the table but I still had doubts about the affect it would have on everyone else.

When we finally made it over to Mayor Bodenheim's house he was outside just piddling around the flower bed it seemed. I was hoping that this would be a quick visit and we could finally head back to the Davis home.

The mayor recognized Dr. Davis and Professor Jones and invited us all to come into the house, I was lagging behind a little ways because I just wasn't used to white men inviting Negro men to come through the front door of his home the way he had opened his up for us. After the mayor got us all seated and comfortable, he called his wife in and let her know that we were in the house, and also gave her the opportunity to meet me. The way she and the mayor behaved you wouldn't think that there were any racial tensions in East Texas. Mrs. Bodenheim brought us a cool glass of water, for which I was greatly appreciative. My mouth was really dry from all the riding we had been doing in Dr. Davis car. I was still thinking about Meagan a lot, but the way the Bodenheim's were treating us, as though we were just like anyone else, I started to get a little lax in my thinking that it might not be so bad, after all, the way people might treat Meagan and me when they found out we were involved in an interracial relationship.

It was starting to get close to dusk and evening time when the mayor got up from where he was sitting and gestured for us to follow him outside. I wasn't at all in a hurry to leave because the southern hospitality shown by the Bodenheim's seemed too good to be true.

When we finally left Mayor Bodenheim's place I felt worn out from all the different places that Dr. Davis had taken me. I notice as we were riding back to Moberly Edition Professor Jones was taking a nap in the back seat of the car. When we pulled up into Professor Jones yard he was still asleep so I took the liberty and started to tap him on his feet until he woke up. Dr. Davis glanced back at him and said "Professor, we made it to our neighborhood now, so take care and we will see you tomorrow." Professor Jones got out of the car moving sort of gingerly because he was just coming out of a good nap, and then he said, "Alright Doc, you and Lemmel please be careful," and then he walked to the door steps of his house.

CHAPTER

10

After The Article Is Printed: The Race Riot in Longview Would Take Place In 1919

Several weeks had gone by since I had arrived in Longview, and I had had the opportunity to spend some time in Kilgore and meet Meagan's family and some her friends, yet I still found myself very afraid to approach her parents and tell them that Meagan and I are romantically involve and that she's pregnant with my baby. I had plenty of things to do to keep me busy because Dr. Davis used his influence in the neighborhood to help me get a job at one of the stores that were located right down the street from where he lived. It was Sunday evening in June and I was just trying to pass some time while I was living at the Davis home when all of a sudden I heard a car speeding up and down the street, or the road and someone screaming from the car saying "Niggers! Niggers! Stay over here in your own neighborhood, because we don't need your kind over where the good white people live."

This would be the first time I had witnessed the racism that was so prevalent in the south, Because of the lack of rain in several days the streets were very dry, so when the speeding car would make U-turns in the middle of the street the dust would be so thick and high you could barely see the car. I was standing on the porch, trying desperately to make out anything about the car, Mrs. Davis came out and said, "Lemmel, I am embarrassed that you had to hear that, but don't worry, all the white people are not like that." Hearing this, I thought to myself that the Reese family living in Kilgore couldn't be like them. Monday was Dr. Davis' day to go to Kilgore and make his normal early rounds and I was to go with him and assist whenever he needed my help.

Meagan also knew that I would be coming to Kilgore with Dr. Davis on Monday to spend some time with her if it was possible. When Dr. Davis and I finally made it to Kilgore on Monday morning I was so anxious to get finished with the clients over on the Negro section of town so I could make my way to visit Meagan. I no longer felt guilty for coming to Kilgore with Dr. Davis and pretending to be interested in starting a practice in Gregg County. Dr. Davis knew all about my plans to marry Meagan and take her back to Chicago. After we had finished up with our clients, Dr. Davis headed over to Meagan's section of town so I would have a chance to visit with her and make the necessary preparations to get her out of Texas. When Dr. Davis and I drove up to the Reese's house it was about 11 that morning and the entire family was outside in the yard. Even though I had met them before I was very nervous about seeing them now.

I let Dr. Davis take the lead and greet them with a loud hello and ask Mr. Reese if everything was okay and healthy at the plantation. Now that Dr. Davis had broken the ice I could follow up with my own hello to everyone including Meagan. I thought that by speaking to everyone, no one would suspect Meagan and me of having a special relationship. Mr. Reese and the family seemed glad to see us. He came out to the car and greeted us before we had a chance to walk up to the house. I was trying not to look at Meagan too much but it seemed to me that she was just keeping her eyes on me, and now I was starting to get very nervous and uncomfortable, bordering on fright. Dr. Davis noticed Meagan and me looking uncomfortable, so he quickly started asking Mr. Reese about the Negro clients he and I had been seeing after. After Mr. Reese and Dr. Davis concluded their conversation, Dr. Davis and I started to get in the car when someone yelled out to us and said, "Wait.... wait!" We both turned around to see who it was, and to my surprise it was Meagan. When I saw her coming I couldn't help but wonder what she could possibly want at this time. When she finally made it out to where we were she reminded me of the celebration her siblings had planned for her parents' anniversary.

Meagan quickly invited the two of us and Dr. Davis' wife, to the celebration. Of course, being naive, and because of my feelings for her I quickly and gladly accepted the invitation. Dr. Davis said, "Meagan, when do you plan to tell your parents about Lemmel." Meagan was staring at me as though I had betrayed her. Dr. Davis let her know that he and Professor Jones has known about the love affair for some time now, and he told her not to worry because they are in support of Lemmel. I never took my eyes off her when he was telling her this and afterward, she looked at me with relief in her eyes. I was so glad to see that the pressure and burden had been lifted from Meagan's shoulders of keeping it a secret from her family and friends East Texas. Dr. Davis told both of us that he didn't think it was a good idea for me to get too close to the family just yet, but if you two feel like it is time, then do what your hearts are telling you to do.

That last statement Dr. Davis made was all the encouragement I needed to go ahead and be with Meagan and her family. I knew Meagan must have had some kind of plan for her to be coming out and inviting us to the celebration the way she did. I was curious to know just what the plan was so I asked her, "Meagan, how are you going to plan this invitation and explain my presence at the celebration?" She smiled for a moment and then she said to me, "Lemmel I am going to tell everyone tomorrow at the celebration." I then responded by asking her did she plan any kind of transportation for me? Meagan looked over at Dr. Davis with that smile of hers and said to both of us "you all will have to make transportation plans on your own, just be over here tomorrow at 5:00pm for the celebration."
I was so excited I forgot that we still had some clients to see before we left Kilgore. I couldn't help but notice that Dr. Davis didn't seem to be excited at all about our invitation to the celebration. He just kind of

smiled and got back in the car so we could drive on down to where the Negro shacks were.

When we were finally alone in the car I said to or I asked Dr. Davis "what do you really think about us going to the celebration on tomorrow?" Dr. Davis would say to me, "Lemmel it's like I said before I don't think that it is a good idea for you and Meagan to tell her family just yet, but if your heart is telling you to go ahead with it, then I will be behind you 100%." Dr. Davis gave me the feeling that everything that Meagan and I had planned was going to work out just fine. I was devising a plan to secretly take Meagan by train to Chicago tomorrow night after the celebration was over. Now that we had finished our work in Kilgore, Dr. Davis and I headed back to Longview. When we made it to Dr. Davis house we could see Professor Jones walking down the street heading our way. Professor Jones, Dr. Davis yelled and said, "Man you wouldn't believe what happen to Lemmel and me while we were over at the Reese place in Kilgore. This is when Professor Jones walked on up to where Dr. Davis and I were. When he got closer, we could see the look of fear in his eyes. He quickly said, "What happened, Cal, what happened?" While I was listening to all of this I was trying to figure out just what Dr. Davis was talking about, but I just wouldn't be able to do it until Dr. Davis answered him and said, "Lemmel and I were invited to go to the celebration of his white girlfriend's parent's anniversary tomorrow."

Professor Jones looked at me with his eyes widened and bucked, and then he looked at Dr. Davis and asked him, "What did she say when you all declined the invitation?" I spoke up and said, "We didn't decline, we accepted the invitation." He looked at us as though we had lost our minds. I could easily tell he didn't like the idea by the way he was acting and assuming that we had declined the invitation. Professor Jones asked Dr. Davis if he could speak privately. "You mean to tell me you're actually going to go and take Lemmel to the Reese's anniversary party?" "Yes, with some reservation, that's my plan."

Mrs. Davis called Dr. Davis to come inside, she needed him. This would give me a chance to talk to the professor alone and get his perspective on us accepting the invitation. The professor said, "Lemmel, I have known Dr. Davis for several years and I know him better than anyone, and I know he would never have accepted that invitation unless it or someone meant a great deal to him." I started to have mixed emotions because I was beginning to feel guilty again about putting Meagan and myself before anyone else, even if meant endangering the people that was taking care of me like I was their younger brother. By the time we had our little talk, Dr. Davis came back outside to where we were, and begin telling us about his son and wife coming in contact with poison ivy out picking the last of the blackberries, and that it was so severe that he was going to have to stay at home for the next couple of days to look after them.

Then he looked at me and grinned and said "Lemmel you don't have to worry about me driving you to Kilgore tomorrow because I've already talked it over with my wife and we agreed to let you use our car to travel to Kilgore." Caught off guard, I was lost for words so I just said okay and walked to the front door and knocked for Mrs. Davis to let me in. When she let me in, I barely recognized her because she was covered, every square inch of skin that showed in poison ivy blotches and white salve Dr. Davis had put all over her, so the healing process could began. She held the screen door so I could come in and said, "Go ahead and wash up and go in to the kitchen and help yourself to the food I cooked for you all this morning." I said to her, "Okay, Mrs. Davis, I really appreciate the way you and Dr. Davis have taken me in and treated me like a family member." She replied, "Lemmel, it's our pleasure to have you stay with us and give us the opportunity to assist you in the orthodontist field and help you in whatever way we can." I smiled and sat down at the kitchen table and began to eat the food she had prepared for us. The moment I sat down Dr. Davis came into the house. I could hear her talking to Mr. Davis. They came into the kitchen where I was and Dr. Davis was telling me about his entire wardrobe that he had in his closet. Then Mrs. Davis spoke and said, "Lemmel, Cal has opened his entire attire to you so you will be able to look the part of a dentist when you attend the party tomorrow evening."

I stood up with a big smile on my face and hugged Mrs. Davis and grabbed Dr. Davis hand and just started shaking it while I thanked them both again for their southern hospitality. When it was finally time for everyone to go to bed, on this particular night, I didn't sleep very well because my anxiety was at an all-time high. I was really nervous thinking about Meagan and me, breaking the news to her parents. Before you could blink an eye it was already morning and I could hear Dr. Davis stirring around in his workshop in the back of the house.

When I got up and washed my face and hands I noticed that it was late in the morning and that I was the last one out of bed, even Dr. Davis' son Calvin Jr. was up before me. When I finished eating I anxiously left the house to go and help Dr. Davis with whatever he was doing. He saw me coming and started smiling and said "Lemmel, we could tell you weren't sleeping very well last night, so did you get your nap out." I replied, "Yes Dr. Davis, but for a while last night I didn't think I was going to ever go to sleep." Then Dr. Davis just shook his head and said "Lemmel I understand your situation and that's why I am going to do whatever I can to help you." I again thanked him, while he washed the car so it would be shiny and clean when I drove it to Kilgore. After we had worked around the house all day I started to concentrate on the celebration and Meagan Reese.

When I finally made it to Kilgore and drove up to the Reese's house, it seemed to be deserted, but before I could turn the engine off I saw someone opening the door and coming out of the house, and, of course, that someone would be Megan. I asked her, "Meagan, where is everyone?" She said, "Lemmel, the celebration dinner won't begin until 6, so everyone is still out back trying to relax and keep cool." I asked her, "Well, Meagan, what are we going to do in the meantime?"

She got in the car laughing, and said, "We've got almost an hour and a half before the celebration begins." I was still somewhat mystified at her coming out and getting in the car the way she did. We sat there for a moment before she told me to start it up and drive down to where the shacks were. I immediately cranked it up and headed towards the plantation shacks. I passed the last shack when she told me to pull over and park under the trees. When I parked, she scooted over to my side and as I put my arm around her, she laid her head on my shoulder. I turned to her and asked if she really thought it was a good idea for her to be seen sitting in a parked car with me. She looked at me smiling, and said "Lemmel, my parents already know that you would be coming over early to attend to some of your Negro clients before you came to the dinner. I can't wait for this party to be over. I can't wait until tomorrow, to get on that train and head back to Chicago. I won't be at peace in my heart, until we are gone from here and can be together without problems." After a few minutes, I said, "I think it's time to go. I'm sure your folks are looking for you, by now."

I started up the car and headed back to the house when all of a sudden rocks and sticks were coming from everywhere it seemed, and white men looked as though they had fallen out of the sky and on to the trail where I was driving the car. When I lifted my head back up from trying to avoid being hit by the rocks and sticks thrown at me there was a man standing in the middle of road right in front of the car. I couldn't tell who it was because of the sack he had pulled over his head, but I knew that he was out to do me harm. I looked over at Meagan and she looked at me with the look of disgust on her face. Without a word, Meagan jumped out of the car and grabbed a big stick and started beating the man with it.

Stumbling back, he tripped and she dove for his head, but before she would be able to pull the sack off his head two other men rushed over and pulled her away. I was sitting in the car frozen stiff and frightened to the point of tears when several white men pulled me out of the car and threw me down on the ground, whipping me with sticks and beating on me right there in the presence of Meagan. Two guys grabbed Meagan, holding her while the others kicked and hit me. I knew if they kept on, it would be too much for her to take, so she began screaming for them to stop. The louder she screamed, the more intense they became on doing some damage. I heard one of the men tell the others to get Meagan back to the house because they were going to lynch a Nigger tonight. I still wasn't worried after hearing them say this because my main concern was for Meagan and our baby she was carrying. One of the men grabbed me from behind with his arm around my neck, cutting off my air, I began to get dizzy and just before I blacked out, a car came shooting toward us and stopped within a couple of feet. The man let me go and I hit the ground hard, but I looked up and it was the sheriff and his deputy coming to save my life. They stopped the lynching and broke up the mob without having any problems. I was arrested for the first time in my life and I was glad I was being taken to jail and not hanging from a tall pine tree. The sheriff ordered me to get in the car and I gladly followed his instructions. When we were driving away, he turned and asked me with a mouth full of chewing tobacco, "Boy, what are you trying to prove to these white people?" Before I could respond to his question, I saw Meagan running alongside the car crying and screaming for the sheriff to let me out, her girlfriends stopped her and I could see them consoling her as he drove me away.

Riding to the jail, the sheriff tells me that he was locking me up for my own protection because if I was out right now the Reese's would have me lynched. I asked him, "Why would they want me dead? I haven't done anything wrong!" He sort of squints his eyes at me and says, "Boy, you just don't understand how the world is here in the south. Niggers don't mix with whites and Whites don't mix with Niggers and that's all there is to it."

When I heard this, I felt in my soul that I would have to give up on ever seeing Meagan again. I laid on the dirty floor and let the tears roll down my face. I was still too naive to realize just how much danger I was in. As I laid there on the floor the idea came to that Meagan and I could hop a train and leave Texas forever. The sheriff left the deputy with the prisoners and went out on patrol. When he returned a few hours later, he had the look of terror on his face. The deputy asked him, "Was everything okay?

You look like you've seen a ghost!" The sheriff looked at him and shook his head as if to say no, everything is not okay, and then he came over to my cell and said, "Lemmel, we're going to have to get you out of here because the Reese's are more furious than ever. I just got the news that they intend to lynch you tonight." I was terrified, but for some reason I became more determined than ever on getting to Meagan and getting us both out of this country. The sheriff told the deputy and me that he had a plan and he begins to explain it to us. He said, "Lemmel, they are going to come in here and take you out tonight, and I do night have the man power to stop them, so the deputy and I are going to pretend to go along with them and as soon as I can get you separated from them I am going to put you on a train headed out of Longview."

While he was talking, my mind was on Meagan and on how I was going to break loose from him as soon as he got me away from the white mob. I sat in the jail for hours it seemed, waiting for the mob to come and take me away. Finally, as it neared 10:00 pm, we could hear them outside.

The sheriff gave them the key to my cell and it looked as though everything was going as planned, when all of a sudden one of the men reached back and hit me square in the nose almost knocking me unconsciousness. The sheriff and deputy held their peace. Now that we had left the jail, stage 2 of our plan kicked in and I told the men holding me hostage that I had to make water and let my bowels move. This gave the sheriff the opportunity he needed to get me away, and get me on a train.

The plan worked perfectly because the sheriff and I were finally alone and I could now make my escape from him and head back to Kilgore and get Meagan. I knew the train would be headed to Kilgore and all I had to do was hop on it and wait for it to stop at Foote Switch and then on to Kilgore. When they discovered my escape the deputy confessed to them that it was all a plan for the Nigger boy to escape from them but the plan to escape from the sheriff was a plan the Nigger had worked out all alone. They knew that I would probably head straight back to Kilgore to get Meagan and that fancy car, but they didn't know for sure so they broke up into groups to search for me with no success.

They knew that the only way I could beat them back to Kilgore was for me to hop a train, so they contacted the men at Foote Switch and told them to hold the train until they could get there. I was in one of the box cars just waiting for the train to make it to Foote Switch. When the train stopped at Foote Switch I thought, "I'm almost there. It won't be long, now and we'll be free." I leaned back and started to relax and that's when I heard the voices of a mob coming down the track heading straight for the box car I was hiding in. I could hear them outside trying to get in and get me, so I sat very still in the corner of the car desperately hoping and praying they would think it was empty and go away to the next one. At about the time I thought they might be giving up the search the door of the car flew open and one of the men yelled to the others, "Everybody come quick! We got him! I found the Nigger." I jumped up and I found myself right back on the floor. I'd been shot in the right shoulder. I was in excruciating pain from the gunshot wound and as I writhed in pain, someone grabbed me by my legs and dragged me out on to the ground.

They spit on me and kicked me while I was on the ground, called me vile names while tearing at my clothes. I fought hard, but it was no use. There were too many hands and too much strength against me. I knew I could only look to my Savior, now and put myself in his hands. The leader of the mob got a rope around my neck and with the help of the others they drug me to the nearest tree, threw the rope around the trunk of the tree and began to wrap it around and around, the noose pulling tighter and tighter around my neck. I felt the impact of one bullet after another hit my body and I began to get dizzy and weak, bleeding out. As the last bit of consciousness left me, all I could think of was the fact that I would never again hold Meagan or see my unborn child.

The End

EPILOGUE

This would be the last night of Lemmel's life, after they whipped him and stripped all of his clothes off, they tied him to a tree and shot him dead like he was a wild dog. After they had murdered him, they laid his naked body alongside the railroad tracks known as Foote Switch so the killing would serve as an example for the other Negroes to stay in their places. After his body was discovered by some of the Negroes he was brought back to Longview and buried. Dr. Davis, Mrs. Davis and Professor Jones took his death very hard. The morning Lemmel's bullet riddled body was found and they were notified. Professor Jones and Dr. Davis took an oath that they were going to get to the bottom of it and let the whole world know about it. Several days would pass before Dr. Davis and Professor Jones would get a lead on who might be responsible for Lemmel's death. As soon as they got the word from some reliable sources, they made a call to the white leaders in Longview asking them and pleading with them to investigate the matter and bring those responsible to justice. As days continued to pass by, Dr. Davis and Professor Jones started to become very discouraged and angry at the local officials for the slothfulness and unconcern they showed concerning the lynching death of Lemmel Walters.

The Professor and Dr. Davis decided that after several days had gone by and no officials were even talking to them, they were going to write about it and send it to the *Chicago Defender*, a Chicago newspaper owned by Robert Abbott, a Negro. The article was published in the paper on July 4, 1919 and distributed in most parts of the United States. After the article had been put in the *Chicago Defender* newspaper and circulated in most parts of the United States some of the White people living in the Kilgore and Longview area were very ashamed and angered at the fact that a young white woman was in love with a young Negro man, and it would tell of his murder by the white men of the county. Another contributing factor to the anger of the whites was the fact that family after family began to leave the Longview area, decreasing the labor force.

During the time after the article was published between July 4th, 1919 and July the 11th, 1919, there were several skirmishes between the whites and Negroes living in Gregg County. This would go down as the bloodiest confrontation ever in Texas between two races of people. According to the interviews taken from the Black people's perspective that had parents living in Longview at that time, they told of the many gruesome scenes of families being buried at night from the killings that were taking place because of what had happened down at Foote's Switch. There were many Negro families ordered out of town, and some of the Negroes in fear of their lives would leave town in the middle of the night, leaving everything they owned including valuable properties and in some cases the men and young boys would leave behind their families forever.

It was known and reported that because of the publication of the article concerning Lemmel and the white lady, two of the white woman's brothers beat

Professor Jones unmercifully on the day of the race riot. On the night and early morning of July 10 and 11, 1919 for the first time since the Civil War Professor Jones, Dr. Davis and several hundred Negro men pledged to fight to the death when and if a white mob would come over to the colored district on the south side of Longview, seeking to find and lynch Dr. Davis and Professor Jones because of their part in publishing of the article.

In one of the skirmishes that followed, Dr. Davis' father-in-law was killed. There would be many young men killed on the night of July, 11, 1919 - both Negroes and Whites. Dr. Davis and Professor Jones were forced to leave Longview forever after the clash with the white mob on July 11th, 1919. It has been said that after Dr. Davis' request of his friend, the legendary mayor of Longview, Gabriel Bodenheim contacted the governor of Texas that over 300 National Guardsmen and the Texas Rangers would come to Longview to restore and bring peace among the races. Longview or Gregg County race relations has been on an upswing ever since.

Foote

Switch

By

Mandel Stoker

I am a 54 year old African American male and I was born in Longview Texas and have lived and attended schools in Rusk County, a county that is adjacent to Gregg County.

Researched and written by: Mandel Stoker

Dear Reader,

I sincerely hope you enjoyed reading this American love story and at the same time learned a bit more about some things that perhaps you never knew of until now. I most certainly did while doing the research and the writing of this story about this beautiful young American couple. "Foote Switch" was based on a true story and real incidents that actually happened in the lives of real people right in our own back yard of East Texas where so many folk call home. It's truly a 1900s Romeo and Juliet love story. After having read this book I hope you leave with two things. One, that you have a better understanding of the African American struggle for racial equality more than 54 years after the Civil War in Longview, Texas Gregg County was real and two that you will discover your own jewel of a story found in the lives of one of your relatives or maybe even hidden in an old box or trunk in the attic of yours or someone's else's home. There would be other cities all over the United States in the year of 1919 that would go up in flames and run red with blood of Americans. History would record these incidents as the "Red Summer" because of the violence, loss of life and bloodshed.

Sincerely Yours,
Mandel Stoker

Researched and Written By Mandel Stoker with all rights reserved by Mandel Stoker.

For Booking Information Contact:

Mandel Stoker: <u>mandelstoker@yahoo.com</u>

Book cover designed by:

Donald W. Burton

Photos and Newspaper Articles from 1919

lmer | Daily | M

GILMER, Upshur County, TEXAS, FRIDAY AFTERNOON JULY 25,

RACE RIOT IN LONGVIEW—TWO WHITE MEN KILLED FOUR NEGROES KILLED

Four Houses Burned; Much Excitement. Hundreds of Shots Fired. Negro Slander of Kilgore Lady Said to Be Cause of Trouble.

Many wild rumors reached Gilmer Friday morning of a race riot in our neighboring town of Longview, in which it was said that two white men and four negroes were killed, and four negro houses burned with the dead negroes therein.

At the time of going to press it was impossible to get particulars, but a seen from over the slander of a Kilgore white woman by a negro writer to a northern paper, and that every man around Kilgore had gone to Longview with a view of avenging the slander.

The names of none of those killed were learned.

A later report said that the two were four white men and two negroes killed.

People are gathering in there from many sections, and there is said to be an effort on foot to get soldiers there.

Another report that has reached here is to the effect that a white man by the name of White, was among those shot.

It is also reported that the trouble grew out of the negro killing near Kilgore some time ago, when a negro was trailed with bloodhounds from a house there, and the negro afterwards killed, when he admitted that he had been in that room.

The negro writer that report of the incident to the northern paper took the position that the

negro was there by invitation reflecting on the honor of the white woman from whose room he was traced by the bloodhounds before he was killed.

WALTON RED TAG SALE COMMENCED TODAY

The Walton Dry Good Co. commenced Red Tag Sale commenced Friday morning, the store having been closed all of Thursday preparing for it.

This sale is the most widely advertised sale of the year in Gilmer, and they past was more generously advertised than usual, advertisements appearing in Pittsburg, Big Sandy, the Echo and a big daily paper. The Weekly Mirror with thousands of circulars distributed over a wide territory adjacent to Gilmer.

It is such advertising that extends the trade territory of Gilmer, getting people in the habit of trading here that have heretofore been going elsewhere and building up the local trade of Gilmer.

This sale started off auspiciously and we have no doubt will reach its climax tomorrow when the country people have had time to read the advertising and set out about it.

It will be noticed that these sales always start just before Saturday, which gives the town people an opportunity to do their trading before that time.

MASONIC LODGE HANDSOMELY FURNISHED

Bethesda Lodge No 169 A. F. & A. M. is one of the most prosperous lodges in the State of Texas.

It is in they new building occupying the second story as an exclusive lodge room, the First State Bank and the Post office occupying the rest the lower part of the building.

The Lodge in now painting and having put in place an entire new set of furniture, consisting of elegant chairs for the presiding officers, with substantial settees for the attending

There are few lodges in the State more durable finished or in better condition financially than the lodge here.

A telephone, microphone and phonograph have been combined by a French inventor to transmit sounds from the hall to distant points or several places at once.

and Saturday ought to be largely given up to the country people who are here for the day only, and as they can't afford to come to town so many days in the week, whereas the town people are contenting and can do their trading that as well any other day

THE Chicago Defender

Founded May 4, 1905, by
ROBERT S. ABBOTT, LL. B.

VOL. XIV. No. 37.

Published by
THE ROBERT S. ABBOTT PUBLISH.. G
COMPANY (Incorporated)

Entered as second class matter February 1,
1906, at the Postoffice in Chicago, Ill., under act
of March 9, 1879.

CHICAGO—3159 State · Tel. Douglas 3339

TERMS OF SUBSCRIPTION (Payable in Advance)—One year, $2.00; six months, $1.25; foreign, $2.50 per year.

POLICE WORK TO KEEP LYNCHING A SECRET

Longview, Tex., July 4.—Despite the fact that every effort has been made by officials here to keep the outside world from learning of the lynching of Lemmel Walters at this place June 17, the news has leaked out. Walters was taken from the Longview jail by a crowd of white men when a prominent white woman declared she loved him, and if she were in the North would obtain a divorce and marry him. No charge was preferred against Walters other than the statement made by the white woman to her personal friends. The woman has been prostrated since the lynching occurred. She is under the care of a physician at Kilgore, Tex., where Walters was arrested prior to being spirited here for "safe keeping."

The sheriff of the jail gladly welcomed the mob, and acknowledged recognitions from the men as they passed in the gate to seize the prisoner. Walters was taken to the outskirts of the town and shot to pieces. His nude form was thrown near the roadside. He was buried by people of his Race. White people here are angered because our people have been leaving this part of Texas in drove, and since this lynching all the farm hands have left.

ROOSEVELT MEMORIAL INSTITUTIONAL TEMPLE

Newark, N. J.. July 4.—The deed for the transfer of the B'nai Jeshurun Temple (Jewish synagogue), 324 Washington street, to the Roosevelt Memorial Institutional Temple, Fast...

MOB FORCES WOMAN TO IDENTIFY MAN

White Hoodlums Carefully Plan Jim McMillian's Death

By W. L. Porter

Tuscaloosa, Ala., July 4.—Driven from his home between the hours of 12 and 1 o'clock Tuesday morning and forced to take cover some three miles distant in the swamps of Tuscaloosa county, was the fate of Mr. George Lightsey, as result of an alleged outrage, supposed to have been attempted on a white woman Monday afternoon about 2 o'clock by an unknown man, the scene of which is said to be some two miles distant from where Mr. Lightsey lives and across the line in Bibb county.

The woman is supposed to be the victim of three attempted assaults. One, and the first, it is claimed, is said to have been attempted by a Mexican, who stole food from her house. "A big, black Negro" is said to have stolen some of her husband's clothing, while a light, brown-skinned man is said to be the one who attempted criminal assault upon her, tearing her clothes.

Describes Attack

Mr. Lightsey painted a very pathetic picture in his description of the affair when he told how he was aroused from his slumber to find an angry mob surrounding his house, demanding him to come out, and threatening his life if he did not be quick about it. When he was first aroused, according to his own statement, several of the men were trying to raise the windows near which he slept, and when he inquired as to what was the matter, he was told that he know what the matter was, and to come out of there right away. He stated further that the excitement grew so great and that the men were making such an effort to get into the house, that he ran down the hall, out through the back door and down a lane, where he made his es-

White

St. James 307 Sc serious on a was th his co

The crowd McKe resider teenth that I to ena men to lea from t to be ably h some ed to drew Breac standei car w men is not Debne they f scalp were

where being

Mr. teen branch the A Friday poured his wi ter-in whom brutal Green county memb he hai the ri him t thems

It i mob i murde of pr Co., farm eight patch that I held i

NEGRO HOUSES BURN IN REPRISAL

(By Leased Wire to New Mexican.)

Longview, Texas, July 11. — Four white men were wounded early today when negroes fired upon a group of whites they had waylaid in the negro section, where the whites had gone in search of a negro school teacher accused of causing the publication in a negro newspaper of a statement derogatory to a young woman of this county.

There were from 12 to 15 white men in the party and they returned the fire so long as their ammunition lasted, after which they withdrew. It was estimated that from 50 to 75 negroes were in the attacking party.

With reinforcements, the whites returned to the scene, but the negroes had dispersed, leaving no indication of casualties among their number. The whites then burned five negro residences.

Search for two negro ring leaders continued today, but otherwise the city was quiet. It was said the authorities expected no further difficulty in handling the situation. Earlier a request for aid had been made to Governor W. P. Hobby.

DENVER STREET CAR

TRADE

TO

According to the East Texas Historical Journal, various reasons contributed to the racial tension in Longview. African American literature, which circulated in the county, encouraged blacks to "push for better treatment." The most influential African American literature to circulate in Longview was The Chicago Defender, a weekly newspaper with nationwide coverage and circulation. The local reporter and newspaper distributor was a man named Samuel L. Jones, who was also a school teacher. At the time, Jones and a thirty-four-year-old black physician, Dr. Calvin P. Davis, were leaders in Longview's African American community. Not long before the riot, the two had urged local black farmers to avoid white cotton brokers and sell directly to buyers in Galveston. Another source of tension was the murder of Lemmel Walters on June 17, 1919. Earlier that month, Walters had been whipped by two white men from Kilgore, allegedly for making "indecent advances" towards their sister. He was then placed in jail, but a lynch mob abducted him on June 17 and killed him. The immediate cause of the riot was an article published in The Chicago Defender on July 5, 1919, about Walter's death, from the African American perspective. The article said that "Walters' only crime was that he was loved by a white woman," and it quoted her as saying that she "would have married him if they had lived in the North." The newspaper continued on, saying she was so distraught over his death that she required a physician's care. The article also said that the sheriff welcomed the white mob which took Walters and killed him.

TWELVE ARRESTS
MEXICO BORDER
FOR SMUGGLING

Brownsville, Tex., July 13.—
Twelve men were arrested by Mexican authorities as a result of a
round-up of food and liquor smug-
glers along the Mexican side of the
Rio Grande between Matamoros, opposite here, and Rio Bravo, opposite
Hidalgo, Texas, yesterday.

One of the prisoners was shot and
killed by a guard while attempting to
escape from the jail at Matamoros.

The arrests were made in effort to
free the border section of an element
said to have been responsible for the
death of several Mexican federal and
state officers.

18

RAILWAY CLAIM AGENTS ASSOCIATION CLOSES SESSIONS

Times-Herald Special

Galveston, Tex., July 12.—The seventh annual convention of the Railway Claim Agents Association of Texas closed here this afternoon after a two days' session with the election of the following officers for the ensuing year:

President, J. H. Schurba, Dallas; first vice president, W. E. Casey,

Texarkana; second vice president, G. J. Reddick, Dallas; secretary-treasurer, Verne Perryman, Houston.

Dr. A. C. Scott, of Temple, chief surgeon of the Gulf, Colorado and Santa Fe railroad, delivered an address at the closing session on "Traumatic Hernia," illustrating his remarks with a number of charts and drawings. A vote of thanks was tendered the doctor at the conclusion of his address.

Galveston was chosen as the city for the next meeting place.

"Call the minute man."—(Adv.)

RANGERS TO BE KEPT ON DUTY AT LONGVIEW

CITIZENS FEAR TROUBLE IF STATE FORCES ARE WITHDRAWN.

Dallas Guardsmen to Be Sent Home and Nacogdoches Company Remains.

Times-Herald Special

Austin, Tex., July 12.—Adjutant General Harley announced tonight, following receipt of a message from Colonel B. F. Smith of the adjutant general's department, that rangers will be left in Longview at least until Tuesday.

The adjutant general said he believed the rangers would be able to handle the situation and that Dallas troops probably would be ordered home late tonight or tomorrow. Nacogdoches guardsmen may be left in Longview until Monday.

Citizens of Longview said, according to the message, they were afraid of trouble if state forces were withdrawn.

Rioting still is running high following yesterday's race riots, it was said.

Texas Rangers on Guard.

Times-Herald Special

Longview, Tex., July 12.—Upon the capable methods of the Texas Rangers probably will fall the duty of preventing a recurrence of yesterday's race riots in which one negro turned overseas soldier was probably fatally injured, three other white men were shot and several negroes probably were wounded.

This was indicated tonight when a message from Austin said Adjutant General Harley was considering withdrawal of part of the state militia here tonight.

Ranger authorities will make every effort to have the squad of eight rangers now on duty here, retained for several days. The eight rangers will remain on the streets after the militia will be forced again tonight...

About twenty-five negroes, picked up by militiamen as suspects and those who appealed to be guards for protection, were to be sent to Dallas tonight, it was reported. Four negroes arrested for local offenses yesterday, immediately after the shooting affray, will be sent either to Dallas or the state penitentiary at Huntsville to prevent danger of trouble...

LANSING ON LIQUIDATION OF WORLD WAR

(Continued from Page One.)

...then cool heads are still a source of apprehension between Poland and Czecho-Slovakia; Hungary is interrupting trade of all Central Europe; the Adriatic problem is still unsolved, as well as the fate of those large territories formerly under the Turks, including especially Asia Minor and Armenia.

Need World Statesmanship.

"World statesmanship will be sorely tried in the next few years. Two things are essential. First, an exact, intelligent, disinterested public opinion, and second, co-operation of the nations. The former is needed both as a check on any sinister purposes, that may crop up and as the great support for common action. The second is especially helpful in...

WACO FIRM SECURES CONTRACT TO FURNISH GROCERIES TO STATE

Times-Herald Special

Austin, Tex., July 12.—Awarding of contracts for supplying state eleemosynary institutions with dry goods groceries and flour have been made by Captain R. L. Pollard, purchasing agent...

The dry goods contracts were awarded to the Sanger company...

Contracts for groceries were awarded to the Abner company...

All bids on packing house materials and products were rejected on the account of unsatisfactory prices. The grant also rejected all bids on coal and fuel oil, as the department offers to contract with the mines rather than through middlemen or brokers.

Did You Know—

—That we MAKE all the Creams and Sherbets we serve at our fountain or send out to your home—we do, and it's all made in our own factory, provided over by an expert, and this factory is always open to anyone interested, in fact it would be a pleasure to have you call and see just...

STATE FAIR OF TEXAS OPENS TH YEAR ON OCT

Thirty-Third Exposition Will Be Known as "Th Victory Fair."

W. H. Stratton   John S. ...
Secretary   Presiden

Dallas, Tex., July 12.—On Oc 4th the gates of the State 33 third exposition. This will be k as "The Victory Fair."

MARTIAL LAW IN LONGVIEW AND GREGG COUNTY

OVER 360 TEXAS NATIONAL GUARD TROOPS IN COMPLETE CONTROL.

KAISER'S AIDS TO BE TRIED BY ALLIES

In the list of Germans to be put on trial for war-time crimes during the world war, issued by the British French and Belgians are found many noted names. (1) General von Bissing, former commander on the Italian front. (2) Prince Rupprecht of Bavaria, one of the former commanders on the western front. (3) General Stackmann. (4) Baron von der Lancken, "murderer of Edith Cavell." (5) Admiral von Capelle, head of the German navy.

Associated Press.

Longview, Texas, July 14.—The situation here today continued quiet, with Longview and the rest of Gregg county under martial law. The mounted cavalrymen of the Texas National Guard under command of Brigadier General R. H. McDill of Dallas, numbering about 120 men, have complete control of the important arrests in connection with the clash between white men and negroes on Friday were expected during the day.

The ninety-seven guardsmen sent here from Dallas, Terrell and Nacogdoches after Friday's clash, were reinforced Sunday by more than 200 guardsmen from Dallas, Greenville, Beaumont, Tyler, Texarkana and McKinney. The reinforcements ordered in as a result of the declaration as a result of the jostling early Sunday of the negro Marion Bush, father-in-law of Dr. S. V. Davis, who is being sought by authorities as an alleged negro ring leader. The whereabouts of Davis and S. L. Jones, another alleged negro leader, still are unknown.

Dash fired upon county officers who went to his home Saturday night to arrest him in connection with the day's trouble but none of the shots took effect. The negro escaped in the darkness and was intercepted near Longview about 2 o'clock Sunday morning by a posse. When called upon to halt Bush attempted to flee and was shot to death.

Several thousand firearms were turned over to the military Sunday upon orders of General McDill that civilian surrender their weapons as a result of the guardsmen and Texas rangers are the only known armed persons in Longview today. County and city peace officers turned in their guns.

Suspect Negroes in Custody.

Associated Press.

Longview, Texas, July 14.—Texas rangers, cooperating with Texas National Guardsmen at noon today had taken several negroes in custody and placed them under guard at the military camp pending examination. Bush was registered in Friday's clash between white and negro will submit to arrest here today. It was authoritatively announced, and will give band to appear at a probable investigation soon. The racial trouble which led to placing Longview and the rest of Gregg county under martial law on Sunday.

The situation was quiet today. Arrests of suspects will be completed before night, it was reported. Negroes to be held for grand jury investigation will be transferred to the jail at some other county, probably Dallas, it was said.

ROYAL HAT CLEANERS.

We clean and block all kinds of straw and Panama hats. Tie and 616 N. ...tt.

KENDALES.

Two-four weeks have delivered advertisers in city limits for 12.50. Phone 1053 or 2545.—Adv.

Kelly-Springfield Tires

Handled and Sold by
HEDRICK HARDWARE CO.
Distributors
(Advertisement.)

SECOND CALLED SESSION THIRTY-SIXTH NEAR END

House and Senate Calendars Promise to Become Graveyard for Bills.

Associated Press.

Austin, Tex., July 14.—With the beginning of the last week of the second called session of the Thirty-sixth Texas legislature, calendars of both the house and the senate promised to become a graveyard, the sixth day of the expiration of the present session at midnight, July 22, at which time this section adjourns under the rule the tax works regulating its sitting.

Governor W. P. Hobby has stated that he will not call another session unless it is necessary for tax fund disposition of appropriations and a few appears to be ended at once, all vehicles must be discontinued before they can be considered.

Which carried the appropriations committees say that the appropriations measures will be disposed of before this second term and certain new provides some of a matter, and under provided necessary enough Hall only, subject of appropriations under will be supported.

HOUSE REFUSES TO VOTE ON REPEAL WAR PROHIBITION

Associated Press.

Washington, July 14.—An attempt to force a vote on repeal of war-time prohibition failed today in the house. On a point of order raised by Chairman Volstead of the judiciary committee an amendment to the pending prohibition enforcement bill proposed by Representative Gard of Ohio, of Missouri, was ruled out of order.

DUST IS STIFLING ON MARY STREET

WILL URGE CLOSE RELATIONS LABOR AND THE FARMERS

A feature of the Central Labor council meeting Tuesday evening at which will be an address by Joe Eanglesby of Waterford on the best kinsmanship of labor and the general closer affiliation of farmers and organized city labor.

Mr. Eanglesby represents the Texas Federation of Texas. He is reported to address the careful sound system of important producers.

The relations his reaction will come up for discussion at this hearing, announces J. B. Harwood, Jr., and president K. W. Danze is regular a full representation of all labor.

Children Cry FOR FLETCHER'S CASTORIA

Waco Soldier Boy Gets Home on First Wedding Anniversary

Times-Herald Correspondence.
Waco, Texas, July 14.—...

'Longview Race Riot' a sa

It was easily the saddest period in Longview's history.

Little, if anything, is spoken now about what became known as the "Longview Race Riot." The events of July 1919 aren't something you'd like to brag about.

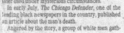

Van Craddock

THE TROUBLE started in June that year when, the story goes, a black man supposedly made advances toward a white woman in Kilgore. The man was brought to Longview, the county seat, and a few days later died under mysterious circumstances.

In early July, The Chicago Defender, one of the leading black newspapers in the country, published an article about the man's death.

Angered by the story, a group of white men gathered at the home of a black school teacher whom they accused of submitting the article to the Defender. On a downtown street, they severely beat the teacher, and then the mood really turned ugly.

THE NIGHT OF JULY 11, 1919, a mob of whites gathered in downtown Longview while blacks began to gather in their part of town. Mayor G.A. Bodenheim and other level-headed civic leaders of both races asked the groups to disband. But Bodenheim and the others were ignored.

Along about midnight, the whites headed for the black teacher's house, ordering him to give himself up. Then a shot rang out — the whites blamed the blacks for firing the first shot, and the blacks blamed the whites — and the riot was on.

MEN FROM BOTH SIDES were armed, and pretty soon Longview sounded like a civil war battle. Some accounts say more than 100 shots were fired.

d period of local history

When the shooting ended some time later, several white men had been wounded.

The city's fire alarm was sounded, and soon a large crowd of whites had assembled downtown. Rifles and ammunition were handed out, and at daybreak the mob again headed toward the black section of town. There the school teacher's house was torched, along with several other structures.

Enough was enough. Local officials phoned Texas Gov. William P. Hobby, who ordered a number of Texas Rangers to Longview as well as some 100 National Guard troops. They arrived July 12 and set up camp on the courthouse lawn.

Early July 13, trouble again flared when a black man and county officers exchanged gunfire. Later that day, the man was killed by "armed citizens," according to one newspaper account. At that point, martial law was declared, and National Guard Brig. Gen. R.H. McDill ordered every firearm in Gregg County to be surrendered to him. Several thousand weapons were turned in, including those of the county sheriff and his deputies.

ON JULY 14, ARRESTS began, and eventually some 50 men, both black and white, were arrested for their involvement in the riot.

On July 15, a citizens' committee adopted a resolution "deploring and condemning the actions of the said negro. . .in circulating the paper containing the scurrilous article" and also "condemning the actions of the white men and boys in setting fire to the houses. . ."

Finally, on Friday, July 18, martial law was lifted and the militia and Rangers left. In an effort to promote better relations between the two races and to put the lawlessness behind them, none of the men arrested were ever tried for their participation in the riot.

Longview was not alone. The summer of 1919 was probably the worst period of racial tension in the nation's history. More than two dozen race riots occurred that summer, including Chicago, Knoxville, and Washington, D.C.

I would like to thank the Genealogy Longview Library and the Chicago Defender for the invaluable articles they provided that was printed in

July of 1919.

I would also like to thank the Longview Museum for providing us with key information and the article provided by Mr. Van Craddock in 1986 concerning the race riot in 1919.

Made in the USA
Middletown, DE
01 December 2018